ALSO BY

JEFF SCOTT

ARCHIMEDES
AND
THE ORDER OF PYTHAGORAS

JEFFSCOTTBOOKS.com

The Mathematician

Jeff Scott

THE MATHEMATICIAN

This work is of fiction. Any references to historical events, real people, or real locales are used fictitiously

Copyright © 2024
First Publication 2024 by KDP

It All rights reserved, including the right of reproduction
In whole or in part in any form

Scott, Jeff
The Mathematician

Book Design and cover concept by
Jeff Scott

*This book is dedicated to two people,
my mother Carole, who was the smartest
person I've ever known. For as long as
I can remember she had a book in her hand.*

*Also to my daughter Tristen
who is basically my mothers clone when it comes to
books.
She's a teacher, like my mom had always wanted to be,
She is always reading and should definitely write a
book of
her own.*

I love you both so much.

Without mathematics, there's nothing you can do. Everything around you is mathematics. Everything around you is numbers.
— Shakuntala Devi, Indian writer and mental calculator

THE MATHEMATICIAN

Prologue

The city at night was a labyrinth of shadows and light, a puzzle of intersecting streets and alleys that concealed both the mundane and the malevolent. In the darkness, a figure moved with calculated precision, a predator on the prowl. He was not driven by rage or desire, but by an insatiable need to solve the ultimate equation—a problem only he could comprehend.

In a dimly lit warehouse on the outskirts of the city, the figure stood over his latest creation. The girl, no more than sixteen, lay still on the cold, concrete floor. Her lifeless eyes stared into the void, reflecting the cruel indifference of her killer. He knelt beside her, his gloved hands meticulously arranging her hair, ensuring every detail was perfect.

From his pocket, he retrieved a small piece of chalk, its surface worn from use. With a steady hand, he began to write on the wall, each stroke deliberate and precise. The equation took shape, a cryptic message left for those who would come after—a challenge to their intellect, a taunt to their inadequacies.

He stepped back, admiring his work. The blood-red symbols stood stark against the grey concrete, a testament to his genius. He felt a thrill of satisfaction, knowing that this puzzle would confound them, that they would struggle to understand the mind behind the madness.

As he turned to leave, the faint sound of sirens echoed in the distance, growing louder with each passing second. He slipped into the shadows, disappearing into the night, leaving behind another

piece of the puzzle for Detective Frank Griffin and his team to decipher.

The chase was part of the game, an intricate dance between predator and prey. He relished the challenge, knowing that with each new victim, he drew them closer to the ultimate truth—a truth they were ill-equipped to grasp.

For Detective Griffin, the pursuit of the "Mathematician Killer" was more than just another case; it was a battle against the darkness that had claimed so many lives, a fight to restore some semblance of order in a world descending into chaos. Little did he know, the path to the killer would lead him to unexpected places, forcing him to confront not only the mind of a madman but also his own deepest fears and regrets.

As the city slept, oblivious to the horrors lurking within, one man remained awake, his mind a web of intricate calculations and deadly intent. The game had begun, and only time would reveal the victor.

In the end, it was all a matter of solving the equation of death.

~ONE~

Insomnia and Equations

Detective Frank Griffin was a man who commanded attention, both through his imposing physique and the weight of his presence. Tall and handsome, with dark hair combed back in a manner reminiscent of the Fonz from *Happy Days*, he had a slender yet muscular build that spoke of discipline and resilience. His face, lined with the worries and wear of years spent solving the darkest of crimes, revealed a life dedicated to the pursuit of justice—a life that had left little room for anything else.

Griffin's apartment was on the 17th floor of a new tower complex, a modern edifice of glass and steel that stood as a testament to the city's relentless march towards the future. His home was a sanctuary of sorts, a beautifully appointed two-bedroom unit with granite countertops and commercial-style appliances in the kitchen. The space was both a reflection of his success and a stark reminder of his solitude. The second bedroom, unused and untouched, symbolized the family visits that never happened.

A widower, Griffin's personal life was as complex as the cases he worked on. He had three adult daughters who loved him but resented the long hours and emotional toll his job demanded. The youngest, Mary, called often, but living across the country meant visits were rare. In the quiet moments, Griffin sometimes wondered

if his daughters' distance was a result of his own doing, the consequence of years spent prioritizing his badge over his family.

At 3:17 a.m., Griffin found himself awake once more, the familiar ache of insomnia gnawing at him. He sat on the balcony, 17 stories above the city's restless pulse, smoking a cigarette and nursing a cup of black coffee strong enough to strip paint. The faint hum of traffic below provided a strange sense of comfort, a reminder that life continued, despite the horrors he confronted daily.

His mind, ever restless, wandered through a labyrinth of thoughts. "What would the Earth fear if it had feelings?" he mused. "Probably us, because we're gluttonous pigs, consuming everything in our path."

Or, "How many possible three-digit combinations are there?" His mind flicked through the permutations— 1000 with repeating digits, 720 without. "10x9x8."

These thoughts weren't random, though. They were echoes of the latest crime scene, a macabre tableau etched into his memory. The last victim, Lisa Davidson, had been found with a math problem scrawled in blood on the wall: a grim signature of the "Mathematician Killer," as the press had dubbed him. Lisa, a beautiful 16-year-old with dark hair and piercing blue eyes, had a promising future stolen from her by a monster who reveled in mathematical sadism.

Lisa was the 15th victim in as many months, each girl marked by their intelligence and potential, each crime scene defiled with blood-soaked equations. Griffin's heart ached for the families, for the futures extinguished before they could fully bloom. As he sipped his coffee—black and thick like crude oil—his thoughts darkened.

"What I'd love to do to this guy in a dark alley," he thought, a cold fury simmering beneath his composed exterior.

The night stretched on, the city below oblivious to the predator in its midst. Griffin knew he had to catch this killer, not just for the victims, but to reclaim a piece of his own humanity lost in the shadows of unsolved cases and sleepless nights. He crushed the cigarette underfoot and took another sip of his coffee, the bitterness matching the resolve in his heart. Tomorrow would bring another day of hunting, another chance to solve the equation of a madman's mind.

~TWO~

The Captain's Lament

Detective Frank Griffin entered the homicide unit's office, a sprawling, chaotic space filled with desks buried under mountains of paperwork, whiteboards scribbled with notes, and the constant hum of voices and ringing phones. The overhead fluorescent lights cast a harsh, clinical glow, adding to the general atmosphere of urgency and fatigue. At the far end of the room was Captain Joe Hogan's office, a glass-walled enclosure that afforded him a clear view of his domain—and the detective he was about to summon.

Captain Joe Hogan was a man whose physical presence did not match his command. Standing at 5'9", with a balding pate and a stocky build, he was far from intimidating in appearance. But when Hogan barked orders, his voice carried the weight of decades of authority and experience. It was a well-known fact around the precinct that the captain had an aversion to the f-word, opting instead for his peculiar exclamation: "What the shit?"

Griffin braced himself as he approached the glass door, knowing full well that today's meeting would be intense. Hogan was already in a foul mood, his frustration palpable from across the room. The door swung open, and Hogan's voice, gruff and strained, cut through the office chatter.

"Griffin! Get your ass in here, now!"

Griffin stepped inside, closing the door behind him. Hogan's office was a cluttered but organized space, reflecting the mind of its occupant. Files and case folders were stacked neatly on his desk, interspersed with photos of his family and commendations from his years of service. A large map of the city covered one wall, peppered with colored pins marking crime scenes. Behind his desk, Hogan sat in a leather chair that had seen better days, its creases and worn patches a testament to long hours and sleepless nights.

Captain Hogan looked up, his face a mask of barely restrained anger. His eyes, usually a calm blue, now blazed with a fury that Griffin had seen many times before but never directed at himself. Hogan's desk was a battlefield of reports, witness statements, and autopsy photos, with the latest case file on top—a stark reminder of their collective failure to catch the "Mathematician Killer."

"Sit down, Griffin," Hogan commanded, pointing to the chair opposite his desk. Griffin complied, feeling the weight of Hogan's gaze on him.

"What the shit is going on with this case, Frank? Fifteen victims, and we're no closer to catching this bastard than we were a year ago!" Hogan's voice rose, echoing through the glass walls and drawing the attention of the detectives outside.

Griffin met Hogan's glare with a steady gaze. "We're doing everything we can, Captain. The killer's smart, methodical. He doesn't leave any useful evidence behind, and the math problems... they're intricate. We're working with experts, but it's slow going."

Hogan slammed a fist on the desk, causing a stack of papers to teeter. "Slow going? Tell that to the families of those girls! Tell that to my sister!" He paused, struggling to regain his composure. "Jessica was only seventeen, Frank. Seventeen. She was my niece and she was just starting her life."

The room fell silent as Griffin absorbed the captain's words. Jessica Hogan had been victim number seven, found in an abandoned warehouse with a bloody equation written on the wall beside her. She had been a bright, ambitious young woman with dreams of becoming a lawyer, a DA because of a long line of lawmen in her ancestry. Her uncle, grandfather and great grandfather had all been cops. She was born out

of wedlock, but her mother did remarry and her stepdad was great. He adopted her, but she kept the name Hogan because she was damn proud of the name
Her dreams were cut short by the monstrous actions of the "Mathematician Killer." Her death had hit the precinct hard, but for Captain Hogan, it was a personal vendetta.

Griffin nodded slowly. "I know, Joe. I remember Jessica. She was a good kid. We'll get this guy, I promise."

Hogan leaned back in his chair, rubbing his temples. "Promises don't bring her back, Frank. I need results. I need this guy off the streets before he kills again. What do we have on him?"

Griffin took a deep breath and began to outline the latest developments—or lack thereof. "We've re-interviewed everyone connected to the victims, re-examined the crime scenes. We're collaborating with mathematicians to decode the equations. So far, we've identified patterns, but nothing that points us directly to the killer. He's careful, leaves no DNA, no fingerprints. The equations are our only lead, but they're like solving a cryptic puzzle."

Hogan's frustration was evident, but he listened intently. "And the profiler?"

"They believe the killer is someone with a high level of education, possibly a teacher or someone in academia. The precision and complexity of the math problems suggest someone deeply familiar with advanced mathematics. But that's a wide net."

Hogan sighed, a heavy sound that seemed to carry the weight of his grief and responsibility. "Frank, we're running out of time. This guy is escalating. Fifteen victims in fifteen months. If we don't stop him soon, there'll be another girl, another family destroyed."

Griffin nodded, feeling the same sense of urgency. "I know, Captain. We're pushing every resource we have. We'll catch him."

Hogan leaned forward, his eyes locking onto Griffin's with a fierce determination. "You better, Frank. For Jessica's sake. For all their sakes."

Jessica Hogan had been an exceptional young woman, a star student with a bright future ahead of her. She had been captain of her high school debate team, an honor student with a full scholarship to a prestigious university. Her ambition was to follow in her uncle's footsteps, but as a prosecutor, fighting for justice in the courtroom.

Her death had been particularly brutal, a stark contrast to her promising life. She had been found in an abandoned warehouse on the outskirts of the city, her body arranged in a grotesque display that haunted everyone who had seen it. The equation scrawled in her blood was a complex calculus problem, one that had taken days for the experts to decode. The solution had been chillingly simple: "Her potential was infinite."

The loss of his niece had shattered Captain Hogan, driving him to a relentless pursuit of the killer. His anger, once a controlled fire, had become a raging inferno of determination. Each new victim was a fresh wound, a reminder of the personal vendetta he carried.

Griffin watched as Hogan tried to contain his emotions, the struggle evident in every line of his face. He knew that catching the killer wasn't just about stopping a madman; it was about bringing peace to his captain, to the families, and to himself.

"We've got another lead," Griffin said, breaking the silence. "A professor at the university thinks the killer might be using a specific mathematical pattern, something called the Fibonacci sequence. We're looking into anyone with a connection to that."

Hogan looked up, a glimmer of hope in his eyes. "Fibonacci sequence? That's the series where each number is the sum of the two preceding ones, right?"

Griffin nodded. "Yes, and it appears in a lot of natural phenomena, but in this case, it might be a clue to the killer's mindset. We're cross-referencing it with known suspects, looking for anyone with an unusual interest or expertise in that area."

Hogan leaned back, his expression thoughtful. "It's a start. Keep me updated on that lead. And Frank, remember—we're all counting on you."

Griffin stood up, feeling the weight of Hogan's expectations and the enormity of the task ahead. "I won't let you down, Captain."

As he left Hogan's office, Griffin felt a renewed sense of purpose. The hunt for the "Mathematician Killer" was far from over, but with each step, they were closing in on their target. For Jessica, for the other victims, and for the peace that had eluded them for too long.

The office buzzed with activity as Griffin returned to his desk, the faces of his colleagues reflecting the same determination that burned within him. They were a team, united by a common goal, driven by the need to stop a monster and restore a measure of justice to a city under siege.

Outside, the city continued its relentless march towards dawn, oblivious to the shadows lurking within. But inside the precinct, a different kind of march was underway—a march towards justice, led by a detective who refused to let the darkness prevail.

~THREE~

The Professor

Detective Frank Griffin entered the imposing building of the city's prestigious university, the stone facade and ivy-covered walls a stark contrast to the gritty urban environment outside. He made his way through the hallowed halls, lined with portraits of esteemed scholars, towards the mathematics department. Today, he was meeting with Professor Wolfgang Einstein, an expert who might provide crucial insight into the case that had haunted him for months.
Einstein is no relation to the famous mathematician, just coincidence they share a name and passion for mathematics.

Griffin knocked on the door labeled "Dr. Wolfgang Einstein, Department of Mathematics." A moment later, the door swung open, revealing a man in his early forties with silvery hair neatly parted to the side and a strong, angular jaw. Standing just shy of six feet, Professor Einstein exuded a calm confidence that came from years of academic achievement. His slight German accent added a touch of old-world charm, a remnant of his early years spent in Europe.

"Detective Griffin, I presume?" Einstein's voice was warm and welcoming as he extended his hand.

"Yes, Professor Einstein. Thank you for agreeing to meet with me," Griffin replied, shaking the professor's hand firmly.

"Please, come in. Make yourself comfortable," Einstein said, gesturing to a pair of leather chairs in front of his mahogany desk. The office was a blend of the old and the new—ancient mathematical texts and modern research papers shared space on the shelves, while framed certificates and awards adorned the walls.

Griffin took a seat, glancing around the room. "This is quite an impressive office, Professor. Your accolades are well-deserved."

Einstein smiled modestly. "Thank you, Detective. Mathematics has always been my passion, ever since I was a child. But please, call me Wolfgang."

"Alright, Wolfgang. I appreciate your time. I need your expertise on a series of mathematical problems that have been left at several crime scenes. We believe they might help us understand the mind of the killer."

Einstein nodded, his expression growing serious. "I've read about the case in the papers. The so-called 'Mathematician Killer.' It's a terrible tragedy. I'll do whatever I can to assist you."

Griffin reached into his briefcase and pulled out a folder, handing it to Einstein. "These are photographs of the equations left at the scenes. They're quite complex, and we're hoping you can shed some light on their significance."

Einstein opened the folder and studied the images carefully. His brow furrowed in concentration as he traced the equations with his finger. "These are indeed intricate. The killer has a deep understanding of advanced mathematics."

"Do you recognize any specific patterns or sequences?" Griffin asked, leaning forward.

Einstein looked up, his eyes bright with excitement. "Yes, this one here," he pointed to an image, "is based on the Fibonacci sequence. It's a series where each number is the sum of the two preceding ones, starting from zero and one. It's a fascinating pattern that appears in many natural phenomena, such as the arrangement of leaves on a stem, the branching of trees, and even the spirals of shells."

Griffin nodded, taking notes. "Can you explain the significance of the Fibonacci sequence in more detail?"

Einstein's passion for the subject was evident as he spoke. "The Fibonacci sequence is named after the Italian mathematician Leonardo of Pisa, known as Fibonacci, who introduced it to the Western world in his book *Liber Abaci* in 1202. The sequence begins with zero and one, and each subsequent number is the sum of the previous two. So it goes 0, 1, 1, 2, 3, 5, 8, 13, and so on."

He paused to ensure Griffin was following. "This sequence is remarkable because it is found everywhere in nature. The number of petals on a flower, the arrangement of pinecones, and the branching of trees often follow the Fibonacci pattern. It's as if nature itself is a grand mathematical puzzle."

Griffin was fascinated. "And how does this relate to the killer's mindset?"

Einstein leaned back in his chair, his fingers steepled. "The killer's use of the Fibonacci sequence suggests an obsession with order and patterns. It's possible he sees his actions as part of a larger, cosmic design, something that transcends ordinary human understanding. This could be a way for him to impose his sense of control and intellect over the chaos of the world."

Griffin considered this. "So, the equations aren't just random. They're part of a larger, deliberate pattern?"

"Precisely," Einstein confirmed. "Each equation likely holds a deeper meaning, a message the killer wants to convey. It's a form of communication, a twisted way of proving his superiority and intellect."

Griffin nodded slowly, absorbing the information. "Can you help us decode the rest of these equations? We need to understand what he's trying to say."

"Of course," Einstein replied without hesitation. "I'll analyze these and see if I can uncover any more patterns or connections. It will take some time, but I'll do my best."

"Thank you, Wolfgang. Any insight you can provide could be crucial in stopping this killer."

Einstein stood, extending his hand again. "I'll start working on these right away. And please, keep me informed of any new developments. This case is...personal for me. Mathematics is a beautiful language, and it pains me to see it used for such darkness."

Griffin shook his hand firmly. "I will. Thank you, Professor."

As Griffin left the office, he felt a renewed sense of hope. Wolfgang Einstein was clearly passionate and knowledgeable, and his expertise might just be the key to unlocking the killer's mind. Yet, there was something about the professor's intensity that lingered in Griffin's mind. He shook off the thought as he made his way back to the precinct, focusing instead on the next steps in the investigation.

Back at the precinct, Griffin briefed his team on the meeting with Professor Einstein. They gathered around the whiteboard, where the equations from the crime scenes were displayed.

"Einstein believes the killer is using the Fibonacci sequence and possibly other mathematical patterns to communicate," Griffin explained. "He's going to analyze the equations in detail, looking for any clues we might have missed."

Detective Sarah Collins, a sharp-minded investigator with a knack for spotting patterns, looked intrigued. "If the killer is using the Fibonacci sequence, there might be a deeper connection between the victims and the sequence itself. Perhaps their ages, locations, or even dates of death follow the pattern."

"Exactly," Griffin agreed. "We need to re-examine everything with fresh eyes. Look for any connections that fit the sequence or other mathematical patterns."

As the team got to work, Griffin couldn't shake a feeling of unease. The killer was clearly intelligent, methodical, and driven by a sense of purpose that made him incredibly dangerous. But for the first time, Griffin felt they had a chance to get ahead of him, to anticipate his next move.

Hours turned into days as the team pored over the evidence, consulting with Einstein regularly. The professor's insights proved invaluable, helping them decode several of the equations and uncovering a chilling pattern: the intervals between the murders were also following the Fibonacci sequence. Each new victim was found after a period of time corresponding to a number in the sequence.

"This means we can predict when the next murder might happen," Collins said, a mixture of excitement and dread in her voice.

Griffin nodded. "Yes, but we need to be ready. The killer will likely know we're onto him and could change his pattern to throw us off."

Einstein, who had joined them at the precinct for the latest briefing, spoke up. "Detective, I've also noticed something else. The locations of the murders form a spiral pattern on the map, which is another characteristic of the Fibonacci sequence. If we can predict the next point on the spiral, we might be able to narrow down the location."

Griffin felt a surge of adrenaline. "Alright, let's get to work on that. We don't have much time."

As they worked tirelessly to predict the next location, Griffin found himself increasingly impressed by Einstein's brilliance and dedication. The professor's passion for mathematics was infectious, and his ability to see patterns where others saw chaos was a crucial asset.

One evening, as they pored over maps and equations in the dimly lit precinct, Griffin turned to Einstein. "Wolfgang, I have to ask—how did you become so fascinated by mathematics?"

Einstein smiled, leaning back in his chair. "It's a long story, but in short, I was always drawn to the beauty of numbers and patterns. Growing up in Germany, I was a bit of an outsider, but mathematics gave me a way to connect with the world. When my family moved to the United States, I skipped a couple of grades and took college courses in high school. Eventually, I attended MIT and earned my doctorate by the time I was twenty-five."

Griffin was impressed. "That's quite an achievement. And now you're helping us catch a killer using those same skills."

Einstein nodded, his expression turning serious. "Yes, it's a strange twist of fate. But if my knowledge can save lives, then it's worth it."

As the night wore on, the team continued their work, driven by the knowledge that time was running out. Each new piece of the puzzle brought them closer to the killer, but also revealed the depth of his cunning and intelligence.

~FOUR~

The Fibonacci Trail

In the early hours of the morning, Griffin received a call. Another body had been found, and the scene was eerily familiar. The killer had struck again, despite their best efforts to anticipate his moves.

Griffin and his team rushed to the location, a secluded park on the outskirts of the city. The area was cordoned off with police tape, and forensic technicians were already at work, their flashlights casting long shadows in the pre-dawn darkness.

Griffin approached the scene with a sense of dread. The victim, a young woman in her late teens, lay on the ground, her lifeless eyes staring up at the sky. Another equation was scrawled on a nearby tree, this time in chalk, glowing faintly under the forensic lights.

He knelt beside the body, his heart heavy with frustration and sorrow. Despite their best efforts, they had been too late. He stood up and walked over to where Einstein was examining the equation.

"This is a new one," Einstein said, his voice tense. "It's based on a different mathematical concept—something more obscure. He's challenging us again, raising the stakes."

Griffin nodded, his jaw clenched. "Can you decode it?"

Einstein studied the equation for a moment before replying. "Yes, but it will take some time. This one is more complex."

Griffin turned to Collins, who was coordinating with the forensics team. "We need to work faster. He's escalating, and we can't afford to fall behind."

As they left the scene, Griffin couldn't shake the feeling that they were missing something—some crucial detail that could unlock the killer's identity. He glanced at Einstein, who was deep in thought, his fingers tapping a rhythm on his notebook.

"Wolfgang, do you think there's a personal connection between the victims?" Griffin asked, breaking the silence.

Einstein looked up, considering the question. "It's possible. The mathematical patterns suggest a deeper significance, something personal to the killer. We need to look into the victims' backgrounds more thoroughly, see if there's a common thread."

Back at the precinct, the team redoubled their efforts. Collins and the other detectives started digging into the victims' lives, searching for any connections that might provide a clue. Meanwhile, Einstein worked tirelessly to decode the latest equation, his mind racing with possibilities.

As the hours passed, a picture began to emerge. Collins discovered that several of the victims had attended the same summer camp as children, a camp known for its advanced math program. This connection, though tenuous, was enough to warrant further investigation.

Griffin looked over the camp's records, noting the names of the staff and counselors. One name stood out—Dr. Heinrich Keller, a renowned mathematician who had mentored many of the camp's attendees. Keller had been known for his unconventional teaching methods and his obsession with mathematical purity.

Griffin called Einstein over. "Wolfgang, do you know anything about Heinrich Keller?"

Einstein's eyes widened in recognition. "Yes, I've heard of him. He's a brilliant but controversial figure in the mathematical community. He believes in the inherent beauty and purity of mathematics, often to the exclusion of human considerations. Why do you ask?"

"Keller was a counselor at a summer camp several of our victims attended. I think he might be connected to our killer," Griffin explained.

Einstein nodded thoughtfully. "It's possible. Keller's influence on young minds was profound. If the killer was one of his protégés, it would explain the mathematical precision and obsession with patterns."

Griffin felt a glimmer of hope. "We need to find Keller and talk to him. He might have insights into the killer's identity."

The team tracked Keller to a small town several hours away. Griffin and Einstein made the trip, hoping to find answers. They arrived at Keller's home, a modest house on the outskirts of town, surrounded by a well-kept garden.

Keller greeted them at the door, his demeanor calm and composed. He was an elderly man with thinning white hair and sharp, intelligent eyes. "Detective Griffin, Professor Einstein, how can I help you?"

"We're investigating a series of murders connected by mathematical patterns," Griffin explained. "Several of the victims attended a camp where you were a counselor. We believe there might be a connection."

Keller invited them inside, offering them seats in his cozy living room. "I'm aware of the case. It's been all over the news. I'm saddened to hear that some of my former students are among the victims."

Einstein leaned forward, his tone respectful but probing. "Dr. Keller, we believe the killer is using advanced mathematical concepts in his crimes. Your influence on these students was significant. Can you think of anyone who might have taken your teachings to such an extreme?"

Keller's expression turned thoughtful. "There was one student... exceptionally gifted, but also troubled. He was obsessed with the idea of mathematical perfection, to the point of disregarding human life. I tried to guide him, but his mind was set."

Griffin's pulse quickened. "Do you have a name?"

"His name was Lars Meier. He was a brilliant mathematician, but he struggled with social interactions. I lost track of him after he left the camp, but I remember he was deeply affected by the loss of his parents at a young age. He might have seen his mathematical pursuits as a way to impose order on a chaotic world."

Einstein took note. "This could be our lead. Thank you, Dr. Keller. We'll look into Meier's background."

As they left Keller's home, Griffin felt a renewed sense of purpose. They finally had a name, a direction. But he knew the hardest part was still ahead—finding Meier and stopping him before he could strike again.

Back at the precinct, the team quickly delved into Lars Meier's background. They discovered that he had changed his name to Lars Miller after moving to the city, making him harder to trace. However, his academic records and sparse work history provided enough leads to track him down.

Griffin and Collins, armed with a warrant, made their way to Meier's last known address. It was a small, unassuming apartment in a run-down part of town. They approached cautiously, aware that their quarry was highly intelligent and potentially dangerous.

As they knocked on the door, there was no answer. They forced entry, their guns drawn, sweeping the apartment room by room. It was sparsely furnished, with mathematical equations covering the walls and notebooks filled with dense, complex calculations strewn across the desk.

In the bedroom, they found a hidden compartment beneath the floorboards. Inside was a collection of trophies from his victims—lockets of hair, personal items, and detailed notes about each murder. It was a chilling confirmation of his guilt.

But Meier was nowhere to be found.

The manhunt for Lars Meier intensified. Griffin coordinated with other law enforcement agencies, issuing bulletins and alerts. They knew he wouldn't stop until he was caught, and the pressure was on to find him before he could claim another victim.

Meanwhile, Einstein continued to analyze the equations left at the crime scenes, searching for any clues that might indicate Meier's next move. He worked tirelessly, his mind racing with possibilities.

One night, as Griffin and Einstein reviewed the latest findings, Einstein had a breakthrough. "Frank, I think I've got it. The next equation points to a location—a specific point in the city where the Fibonacci spiral converges."

Griffin's eyes widened. "Can you pinpoint it?"

Einstein nodded, showing Griffin the map. "Here. It's an abandoned warehouse near the docks. If my calculations are correct, that's where he'll strike next."

Griffin didn't waste a moment. He rallied his team, coordinating a raid on the warehouse. They moved in with precision, surrounding the building and cutting off any potential escape routes.

Inside, they found Meier, his eyes wide with a mixture of fear and defiance. He had another victim— a young woman—tied up and unconscious, but still alive. Griffin and his team moved quickly, subduing Meier and freeing the girl.

As they led Meier away in handcuffs, Griffin felt a wave of relief. The nightmare was over. They had caught the killer.

In the aftermath, Griffin and his team received commendations for their work. But Griffin knew that the real heroes were the victims who had unwittingly contributed to the puzzle that led to Meier's capture.

As he stood in his office, looking out over the city, Griffin thought about the strange twists of fate that had brought him to this moment. The battle against darkness was never truly over, but for now, they had won a significant victory.

And he knew that, thanks to the brilliance of minds like Wolfgang Einstein, they would continue to bring light to the darkest corners of the human soul.

~Five~

The Unexpected Twist

Detective Frank Griffin returned to the precinct with a sense of triumph. Lars Meier, who had changed his name to Lars Miller, was in custody, and the young woman he had abducted was safe. The team felt a rare moment of relief, believing they had finally caught the elusive "Mathematician Killer." However, the euphoria was short-lived.

The morning after Meier's arrest, Griffin sat in his office, poring over the details of the case. Something wasn't sitting right with him. The victims of the Mathematician Killer were all teenage girls, yet the young woman they had saved was older, in her mid-thirties. This discrepancy nagged at Griffin's mind, refusing to be ignored.

He called Detective Sarah Collins into his office. "Sarah, I need you to re-examine the profiles of all the victims. Focus on their ages and any other similarities they might share."

Collins nodded, understanding the gravity of the request. "You think we might have the wrong guy?"

Griffin sighed, rubbing his temples. "I'm not sure yet. But something doesn't add up. If we missed something, we need to catch it before another innocent life is lost."

Collins left to gather the necessary files, while Griffin reached out to Professor Wolfgang Einstein. The professor had been instrumental in decoding the equations and identifying the mathematical patterns in the murders. Griffin trusted his analytical mind to help solve this new puzzle.

Einstein arrived at the precinct an hour later, his demeanor as calm and composed as ever. "Detective Griffin, what seems to be the issue?"

Griffin briefed Einstein on his concerns. "Lars Meier's victims were all over the age of thirty, and his methods were different from those of the Mathematician Killer. We might have stopped a killer, but he might not be the one we're looking for."

Einstein nodded thoughtfully. "The mathematical precision and patterns we identified don't align with Meier's modus operandi. It's possible he was inspired by the Mathematician Killer but is not the original perpetrator."

Collins returned with a stack of files. "Here are the profiles, Frank. Let's see if we can find any patterns."

The three of them spent the next few hours meticulously reviewing the information. As they worked, a clearer picture began to emerge. Meier's victims had no connection to the Fibonacci sequence or the mathematical equations left at the crime scenes. Instead, his killings seemed motivated by personal vendettas and a desire for control over his victims.

Griffin's heart sank. "We've stopped Meier, but the real Mathematician Killer is still out there. We need to start from scratch and re-evaluate everything."

Einstein leaned forward, his expression intense. "We should focus on the equations and the specific patterns they follow. There must be a clue we've overlooked."

As the days passed, the team worked tirelessly to uncover any new leads. Collins and the other detectives re-interviewed witnesses and re-examined evidence, while Einstein delved deeper into the mathematical puzzles left by the killer.

One evening, as Griffin and Einstein reviewed their findings, Einstein had a breakthrough. "Frank, I believe I've found something. The intervals between the murders follow the Fibonacci sequence, but there's an additional layer—a hidden code within the equations themselves."

Griffin's eyes widened. "A hidden code? What does it say?"

Einstein pointed to a series of numbers embedded within the equations. "These numbers correspond to coordinates. The killer has been leaving a trail, marking specific locations that form a larger pattern."

Griffin leaned over the map, where Einstein had plotted the coordinates. "It's like a constellation. But what's the significance of these locations?"

Einstein studied the map carefully. "Each location corresponds to a significant mathematical landmark—libraries, research centers, and universities known for their contributions to mathematics."

Griffin felt a chill run down his spine. "The killer is leading us to these places for a reason. We need to visit each one and see if there's a connection."

The next morning, Griffin, Collins, and Einstein set out to visit the first location on the map—a renowned library with an extensive collection of mathematical texts. As they walked through the aisles, Griffin couldn't shake the feeling that they were being watched.

Einstein led them to a section dedicated to mathematical history. "This is where the coordinates pointed. Let's see if there's anything unusual."

They searched the shelves, examining the books and looking for any clues. After an hour, Collins called out, "I think I've found something."

Griffin and Einstein hurried over. Collins was holding an old, leather-bound book. "This book has a hidden compartment in the back. It's been tampered with."

Inside the compartment was a piece of paper with a series of equations and a message: "The answers lie within the patterns. Follow the sequence to find the truth."

Griffin's heart raced. "The killer is taunting us, but he's also giving us clues. We need to keep moving."

They visited the next location, a prestigious university known for its mathematics department. There, they found another hidden message, this time embedded within a mural of famous mathematicians. The message read: "The spiral continues. Can you keep up?"

Einstein analyzed the new equations and determined the next set of coordinates. As they followed the trail, it became clear that the killer was playing a game of cat and mouse, challenging them to keep pace with his twisted intellect.

The trail led them to a secluded research center on the outskirts of the city. As they approached the building, Griffin's instincts went on high alert. The center was abandoned, its windows boarded up and its entrance covered in graffiti.

"This is it," Griffin said, his voice tense. "Be ready for anything."

They entered the building cautiously, flashlights cutting through the darkness. The air was thick with dust, and the silence was oppressive. They moved through the hallways, searching for any sign of the killer.

In one of the rooms, they found a makeshift office with walls covered in equations and photographs of the victims. In the center of the room was a table with a single chair, facing a large whiteboard filled with complex calculations.

Einstein examined the equations, his eyes narrowing. "These are different from the previous ones. More advanced, more intricate."

Griffin scanned the room, his eyes landing on a stack of files. He picked one up and flipped through it. "These are detailed profiles of each victim. He's been studying them, planning every move."

Collins pointed to a series of photographs pinned to the wall. "These are surveillance photos of us. He's been watching us, tracking our progress."

Griffin's blood ran cold. "He's been one step ahead this whole time. We need to find him before he strikes again."

As they continued to search the building, they found a hidden basement. The door was locked, but Griffin forced it open. Inside, they discovered a dark, cavernous room filled with mathematical models and diagrams.

At the far end of the room was a large chalkboard with a single equation written on it. It was a complex, unsolved problem that had stumped mathematicians for centuries.

Einstein approached the chalkboard, his eyes widening in recognition. "This is the Riemann

Hypothesis. It's one of the most famous unsolved problems in mathematics."

Griffin frowned. "What does it mean?"

Einstein turned to face him, his expression grim. "The killer is challenging us to solve it. He believes that by solving this problem, we will understand his motives and his next move."

Collins looked puzzled. "But why? What's the connection?"

Einstein shook his head. "I don't know yet. But this equation is the key. We need to solve it to stop him."

The team returned to the precinct, where Einstein began working on the Riemann Hypothesis with renewed determination. Griffin and Collins continued their investigation, looking for any new leads that might point to the killer's identity.

As the days passed, Einstein made significant progress. He discovered that the killer's equations contained subtle hints and clues that, when deciphered, revealed a hidden message.

Griffin and Collins worked tirelessly to piece together the clues. They interviewed former students and colleagues of Heinrich Keller, hoping to find a connection to the real Mathematician Killer.

One name kept coming up—a brilliant but reclusive mathematician named Dieter Braun. Braun had studied under Keller and had shown a particular interest in the Fibonacci sequence and other mathematical patterns.

Griffin felt a surge of hope. "We need to find Dieter Braun. He could be our guy."

The search for Dieter Braun led them to a remote cabin in the woods, far from the city. As they approached, Griffin felt a sense of urgency. They needed to capture Braun before he could claim another victim.

The cabin was quiet, its windows dark. Griffin, Collins, and a team of officers surrounded the building, their weapons drawn. Griffin knocked on the door, his voice firm. "Dieter Braun, this is the police. We need to talk to you."

There was no response. Griffin motioned for the officers to breach the door. They entered the cabin cautiously, their flashlights cutting through the dim light.

Inside, they found Braun sitting at a desk, his back to them. He was scribbling equations on a piece of paper, seemingly oblivious to their presence.

Griffin approached him slowly. "Dieter Braun, you're under arrest for the murders of multiple individuals. Put your hands where I can see them."

Braun turned slowly, his eyes vacant and detached. "You don't understand. The equations, they're everything. They're perfection."

Griffin approached cautiously. "Mr. Braun, we're taking you into custody. We need to ask you some questions."

As the officers secured Braun, Griffin scanned the room. There were stacks of papers, notebooks filled with mathematical equations, and diagrams plastered across the walls. It was clear that Braun was deeply obsessed with mathematics, but something felt off. The patterns and symbols, while intricate, lacked the precision and thematic consistency of the Mathematician Killer's work.

Collins approached Griffin, concern etched on her face. "Frank, I'm not sure about this. His work doesn't match the killer's style."

Griffin nodded, his instincts telling him the same. "We'll take him in for questioning, but we need to keep digging. There's more to this than we're seeing."

Back at the precinct, Braun was placed in an interrogation room. Griffin and Collins prepared to question him, hoping to extract any useful information that could lead them closer to the real killer.

As they entered the room, Braun sat calmly, his eyes focused on the table. Griffin started the questioning. "Mr. Braun, we're investigating a series of murders connected by complex mathematical equations. Can you tell us about your interest in these patterns?"

Braun's eyes flickered with a hint of recognition. "The Fibonacci sequence, the golden ratio, they're the foundation of everything. But I haven't harmed anyone. I've been here, working on my theories."

Griffin exchanged a glance with Collins before continuing. "We found your name in connection with Heinrich Keller's former students. Several of the victims attended the same camp where Keller taught. Can you explain that?"

Braun's expression remained blank. "Keller taught me everything I know about mathematics. But I haven't seen him or any of the others in years. My work is solitary. Pure."

Collins leaned forward, her voice gentle but firm. "Mr. Braun, the killer has been leaving mathematical clues at each crime scene. Do you have any idea who could be behind this?"

Braun shook his head slowly. "I've heard about the murders, seen the news. But it's not me. I swear. The equations, they're... they're not right. They're brilliant, yes, but there's a madness to them. A darkness."

Griffin felt a shiver run down his spine. Braun's words resonated with a truth he couldn't ignore. "We need to verify your alibis, Mr. Braun. For now, you'll remain in custody."

As they left the room, Collins sighed. "Frank, I think he's telling the truth. His obsession is with the purity of mathematics, not with killing."

Griffin nodded. "I agree. But if Braun isn't the killer, then we're back to square one. And the real killer is still out there."

The next few days were a flurry of activity. Collins and the other detectives continued to follow up on leads, while Einstein resumed his analysis of the latest clues. Despite their efforts, the sense of urgency and frustration grew. Each day that passed without a breakthrough was a day closer to another potential murder.

One evening, Griffin and Einstein were working late in the precinct, surrounded by stacks of files and crime scene photos. Einstein was deep in thought, his fingers tapping a rhythmic pattern on the desk.

Griffin glanced at him, noting the intense focus in his eyes. "Wolfgang, any new insights?"

Einstein looked up, a faint smile on his lips. "I believe I've found another layer to the equations. It's subtle, but there's a recurring theme—a reference to prime numbers. The killer is using prime numbers to encode locations and times."

Griffin leaned forward, intrigued. "Prime numbers? How does that help us?"

Einstein explained, pointing to a series of equations. "If we map out the prime numbers and the locations of the murders, we can predict where he might strike next. It's a pattern within the pattern."

Griffin felt a surge of hope. "Let's do it. We need to be ready."

The next morning, armed with Einstein's new analysis, Griffin and Collins assembled their team. They mapped out the potential targets, identifying several locations that fit the prime number pattern. They decided to set up surveillance and stakeouts, hoping to catch the killer in the act.

One of the locations was an old observatory on the outskirts of the city. It had been abandoned for years but still held a certain allure due to its history and architectural beauty. Griffin and Collins decided to focus their efforts there, coordinating with other teams to cover the additional locations.

As night fell, Griffin and Collins took their positions near the observatory, their eyes scanning the area for any signs of movement. The air was thick with tension, each minute stretching into what felt like an eternity.

Hours passed without any activity. Griffin's mind raced, replaying the clues and the patterns, searching for any detail they might have missed. Just as he was about to suggest they regroup, a shadow moved near the entrance of the observatory.

Griffin signaled to Collins, and they moved in silently, their hearts pounding. As they approached, they saw a figure entering the building, carrying a large bag. They followed, their steps careful and quiet.

Inside, the observatory was dark and filled with the eerie silence of abandonment. They could hear the faint sound of the figure's footsteps ahead, leading them deeper into the building. Griffin's grip tightened on his weapon, every sense on high alert.

Suddenly, the figure stopped and turned. It was a young man, barely out of his twenties, with a wild, desperate look in his eyes. He dropped the bag, which clattered to the floor, spilling its contents—math textbooks, notebooks filled with equations, and a set of tools.

Griffin and Collins trained their flashlights on him. "Police! Don't move!"

The man raised his hands, his expression one of resigned defeat. "I knew you'd find me eventually. But I'm not who you think I am."

Griffin stepped forward, his voice firm. "Who are you?"

The man took a deep breath. "My name is Felix Meyer. I'm a student, a mathematician. I've been following the murders, trying to decode the killer's patterns. I thought I could stop him."

Collins lowered her weapon slightly. "You're not the killer?"

Meyer shook his head vehemently. "No, no. I've been trying to understand his mind, to find a way to predict his next move. But I'm always one step behind."

Griffin's mind raced. "Why were you here?"

Meyer's eyes widened with fear and desperation. "I thought this was the next target. I've been tracking the patterns, just like you. I wanted to be here, to stop him if I could."

Griffin exchanged a glance with Collins. This young man's story was plausible, but they needed to verify it. "You're coming with us, Meyer. We need to ask you some questions."

Back at the precinct, Meyer was placed in a separate interrogation room. Griffin and Collins reviewed his background, finding no criminal record and a promising academic career. They decided to question him further, hoping to gain more insights into his connection to the case.

As they entered the room, Meyer looked up, his expression a mix of relief and apprehension. "Please, you have to believe me. I'm not the killer."

Griffin nodded, taking a seat across from him. "We're not here to accuse you, Felix. We need your help. Tell us everything you know about the murders and the patterns you've been following."

Meyer took a deep breath, gathering his thoughts. "I've always been fascinated by mathematics, especially the Fibonacci sequence and prime numbers. When I heard about the murders, I saw the patterns immediately. I started tracking them, trying to predict where the killer might strike next."

Collins leaned forward. "Why didn't you come to the police earlier?"

Meyer's eyes filled with regret. "I thought I could handle it on my own. I didn't want to be dismissed as some crazy conspiracy theorist. But I was wrong. I've been trying to stop him, but I've always been too late."

Griffin felt a twinge of sympathy. "We understand, Felix. But we need to know—did you find anything that could lead us to the killer?"

Meyer nodded eagerly. "Yes. The prime number pattern, it's more than just locations. It's a timeline. The killer is following a specific sequence, and I think I've identified the next potential target."

Griffin's heart raced. "Where?"

Meyer pulled out a map and pointed to a location—a high school known for its advanced mathematics program. "Here. The next prime number in the sequence corresponds to this school. If my calculations are correct, he'll strike there soon."

Griffin stood up, determination in his eyes. "We need to move fast. Collins, get the team ready. We're going to that school."

The team arrived at the high school just before dawn, setting up a discreet perimeter. They coordinated with the school administration to ensure the safety of the students and staff while maintaining a low profile to avoid causing panic.

Griffin and Collins took positions inside the school, blending in with the early morning activity. They kept a watchful eye on anyone entering or leaving, ready to act at a moment's notice.

Nothing.... Another dead end.

~SIX~

The Medical Examiner

Detective Frank Griffin sighed deeply as he sat at his cluttered desk, rubbing his temples. The chaos of the precinct buzzed around him, phones ringing, officers talking, the hum of activity a constant background noise. The "Mathematician Killer" case was still the priority, but the homicide unit couldn't afford to focus solely on one case. Two unrelated murders had landed on his desk that morning, further straining their resources and patience.

The first case was a domestic dispute turned fatal. A young couple in their late twenties had been found dead in their apartment. The scene was a mess of shattered glass and broken furniture, indicative of a violent struggle. Neighbors reported hearing yelling and then silence. The husband had a history of aggression, but the details were murky.

The second case was a hit-and-run. A middle-aged man, a well-respected local business owner, had been struck by a car late at night while jogging. Witnesses saw a dark sedan speeding away, but no one could identify the driver or the license plate.

Griffin sighed again, this time more heavily. "It's going to be a long day," he muttered.

As he prepared to head out to the crime scenes, he received a call from the medical examiner's office. Dr. Olivia Brooks, the medical examiner, had requested to see him. Griffin couldn't help but feel a slight flutter in his chest. Dr. Brooks was unlike anyone he had met in his 30-plus years on the force.

Dr. Olivia Brooks was in her early forties, with an appearance that seemed straight out of a classic film noir. She had shoulder-length, chestnut-brown hair that she often wore up in a messy bun, and a pair of thick-rimmed glasses that gave her a librarian-like appearance. Despite her nerdy demeanor, there was an undeniable air of confidence and subtle sensuality about her. She moved with a grace and precision that hinted at her intelligence and meticulous nature.

Griffin found himself drawn to her, though he was aware of the age gap. She was fifteen years his junior, but her maturity and the passion she exuded for her work made her seem older in some ways, a perfect match for his world-weary outlook.

When Griffin arrived at the medical examiner's office, Dr. Brooks was bent over a table, examining a set of gruesome photographs. She looked up as he entered, her eyes lighting up with recognition.

"Detective Griffin," she greeted him warmly. "Thanks for coming."

"Dr. Brooks," Griffin nodded, attempting to keep his tone professional. "You had something you wanted to discuss?"

She gestured for him to join her at the table. "Yes, it's about the Mathematician Killer case. I've been going over the evidence, and I found some inconsistencies that might be important."

Griffin leaned in, his interest piqued. "What have you found?"

Dr. Brooks pointed to the photos. "I've been examining the wounds and the murder weapons used. While the initial assumption was that the killer uses the same type of weapon for each murder, I've discovered that's not the case. The weapons vary significantly. Some victims were stabbed, others were bludgeoned, and one was strangled."

Griffin frowned. "So, he's not consistent with his weapons. What about the equations?"

Dr. Brooks adjusted her glasses, her eyes narrowing as she focused on another set of photos. "That's another interesting point. The equations left at the crime scenes are written in two different mediums—

red chalk and blood. I believe this is a deliberate attempt to confuse us, to make the pattern less discernible."

Griffin rubbed his chin thoughtfully. "Why would he go to such lengths to confuse us?"

Dr. Brooks leaned closer, her voice lowering as if she were sharing a secret. "I think it's part of his game. He wants us to chase our tails, to waste time and resources. He enjoys the chaos he creates, and the more confused we are, the more control he feels he has."

Griffin nodded slowly, processing this new information. "This changes things. We'll need to look at the case from a different angle."

Dr. Brooks smiled, a glint of admiration in her eyes. "I knew you would understand, Detective. You're one of the few who can see the bigger picture."

Their eyes met, and for a moment, Griffin felt a connection that went beyond their professional relationship. He quickly looked away, focusing on the photos again.

"Thank you, Dr. Brooks. Your insights are invaluable," he said, clearing his throat.

"Anytime, Detective," she replied, her smile lingering as he turned to leave.

As Griffin walked back to his desk, his mind was a whirlwind of thoughts. Dr. Brooks' revelations meant they were dealing with a far more complex killer than they had initially thought. The Mathematician Killer was not only brilliant but also highly manipulative, using misdirection as a weapon just as lethal as any knife or gun.

Griffin called Collins and briefed her on what Dr. Brooks had discovered. "We need to re-examine everything," he said. "The weapons, the mediums for the equations, all of it. He's playing a game, and we need to start thinking like him if we're going to catch him."

Collins nodded, her expression determined. "I'll get the team on it. We'll comb through the evidence again, piece by piece."

As the day wore on, Griffin found himself thinking about Dr. Brooks more than he cared to admit. Her intelligence, her confidence, and the way she seemed to understand the complexities of the case in a way few others did—it was all incredibly attractive to him. He shook his head, trying to focus on the task at hand. There would be time to explore those feelings later, once the killer was behind bars.

Over the next few days, the homicide unit worked tirelessly, re-evaluating the evidence with fresh eyes. They cross-referenced the different types of weapons used and the locations where the equations were left, searching for any pattern or clue they might have missed.

Meanwhile, the other two cases—the domestic dispute and the hit-and-run—were progressing slowly. The domestic case seemed straightforward, with the husband's history of aggression making him the prime suspect, but the hit-and-run was proving more challenging, with few leads to go on.

Griffin found himself buried in paperwork and case files, but his mind kept drifting back to Dr. Brooks' office and their conversation. He decided to take a break and visit her again, hoping to discuss the case further and perhaps see her outside of the professional setting.

When he arrived at the medical examiner's office, Dr. Brooks was in the middle of an autopsy, her focus intense as she worked. Griffin waited patiently, admiring her precision and dedication. When she finally noticed him, she smiled and motioned for him to wait a moment.

After she finished, she joined him in her office, closing the door behind her. "Detective Griffin, what brings you back so soon?"

Griffin shrugged, trying to appear casual. "I wanted to discuss the case some more, and... maybe take you out for a coffee, if you're free."

Dr. Brooks raised an eyebrow, a playful smile tugging at her lips. "Detective, are you asking me on a date?"

Griffin felt his cheeks warm. "Maybe I am. If you're interested."

She considered him for a moment before nodding. "I think I'd like that. Coffee sounds great."

As they walked out of the precinct together, Griffin couldn't help but feel a sense of anticipation. The case was far from solved, but for the first time in a while, he felt a glimmer of hope—both professionally and personally.

~SEVEN~

Slow Burn

As the weeks dragged on, Detective Frank Griffin found himself increasingly ensnared in the labyrinth of the Mathematician Killer case. Every spare moment was devoted to poring over evidence, chasing leads, and trying to make sense of the cryptic messages left behind by the elusive murderer. Amidst the chaos of the investigation, a delicate dance began to unfold between Griffin and Dr. Olivia Brooks.

Their encounters were fleeting yet charged with an undeniable electricity that crackled in the air between them. In the rare moments of respite from their relentless work, Griffin found himself drawn to Olivia's company like a moth to a flame. Their dinners together became a sanctuary of sorts, a brief reprieve from the darkness that shadowed their lives.

Olivia, with her intoxicating blend of intelligence and allure, exuded a magnetic pull that Griffin found impossible to resist. Her presence was a balm to his weary soul, her laughter a melody that echoed in the recesses of his mind long after they parted ways.

It was on one such evening, as they sat across from each other in a dimly lit restaurant, that Griffin's gaze lingered a fraction too long on Olivia's form-fitting blouse, which hinted at the curves beneath. He couldn't help but notice the subtle swell of her breasts, the tantalizing glimpse of cleavage that sent a jolt of desire coursing through him.
She had the figure of a 20 something. Never married, no kids and a life of fitness. She does CrossFit 4 times a week and it shows. Frank is no slouch, he's lifted weights at home his entire adult life. They're a good looking couple.

Olivia caught his gaze and smiled knowingly, a mischievous glint dancing in her eyes. She leaned in closer, her voice low and husky with suggestion. "Like what you see, Detective?"

Griffin cleared his throat, a flush creeping up his neck. "I, uh... I'm sorry, Olivia. I didn't mean to..."

Her laughter was like music to his ears, a sweet melody that soothed his frayed nerves. "Relax, Frank. It's just a shirt."

But it wasn't just a shirt, and they both knew it. The tension between them simmered just below the surface, threatening to ignite into something neither of them could control.

As the days turned into weeks, the slow burn of their attraction intensified, fueled by stolen glances and fleeting touches that left Griffin's skin tingling with awareness. He found himself longing for the moments when they were alone, when the outside world faded away and it was just the two of them, suspended in a bubble of desire.

But amidst the growing intimacy between them, there was a shadow looming on the horizon. Einstein's impending departure cast a pall over their budding relationship, a reminder of the fragile nature of their connection.

It was on a warm May evening, as they sat on Olivia's balcony, sipping wine and watching the sun dip below the horizon, then Einstein called and dropped the bombshell.

"I'm leaving for Germany," he announced, his voice tinged with regret. "Family matters. I'll be gone for a few months."

Griffin felt a pang of disappointment at the news, though he tried to hide it behind a mask of indifference. "I see. Well, I hope everything's okay."

Einstein, his expression somber. "Thanks, Frank. It's just... something I have to do."

As Griffin thought of the professor leaving, a sense of foreboding settled over him like a shroud. With Einstein gone, the weight of the case would fall squarely on his shoulders, leaving little time for anything else.

But as he turned to Olivia, her eyes shining with unspoken desire, Griffin knew that whatever lay ahead, he wouldn't be facing it alone. In her arms, he found solace from the storm raging within, a beacon of light in the darkness that threatened to consume them both.

~EIGHT~

Unveiling Desires

After months of relentless pursuit, the precinct finally found itself in a lull. The Mathematician Killer seemed to have vanished into thin air, leaving behind an eerie silence that hung heavy in the air. For Detective Frank Griffin, the respite was a welcome relief from the constant pressure and stress of the case.

With the calm came a newfound sense of freedom—a chance to breathe, to live, to indulge in the pleasures that had been put on hold for far too long. And at the center of it all was Olivia, a beacon of light in the darkness, whose presence brought warmth and joy to Griffin's life.

Their relationship had blossomed over the past few months, growing from cautious flirtation to something deeper and more profound. Their dinners together had become a regular occurrence, a ritual that they both looked forward to with eager anticipation.

Griffin found himself drawn to Olivia in ways he had never experienced before. There was an intensity to her, a fire that burned bright and fierce, igniting something primal within him. And as they sat across from each other, sharing stories and laughter, Griffin couldn't help but marvel at the depth of his feelings for her.

One evening, as the sun dipped below the horizon and the city lights twinkled in the distance, Olivia suggested they retreat to her apartment for a nightcap. Griffin readily agreed, his pulse quickening at the thought of being alone with her.

As they entered her apartment, Griffin was struck by the intimacy of the space—the soft lighting, the plush furniture, the faint scent of her perfume lingering in the air. He felt a rush of desire wash over him, a hunger that he could no longer ignore.

Olivia poured them each a glass of wine and motioned for Griffin to join her on the couch. They sat in comfortable silence for a moment, savoring the warmth of each other's presence.

And then, without warning, Olivia leaned in and pressed her lips to his, a soft, lingering kiss that sent a shockwave of pleasure coursing through Griffin's veins. He responded eagerly, his hands finding purchase in her silky hair as he deepened the kiss, exploring the depths of her mouth with a hunger that bordered on desperation.

Their kisses grew more urgent, more passionate, until they were both gasping for air, their bodies pressed together in a tangle of limbs and desire. Griffin felt a fire ignite within him, a primal need to possess her completely, to lose himself in the heat of their passion.

With trembling hands, he began to explore her body, tracing the curves of her hips, the swell of her breasts, the softness of her skin beneath his fingertips. Olivia moaned softly, her breath hot and heavy against his neck as she arched into his touch, her body humming with anticipation.

Griffin felt a surge of arousal course through him, a hunger that threatened to consume him whole. He wanted her—all of her, completely and unequivocally. And as their desire reached its peak, he knew that there was no turning back.

With a newfound urgency, Griffin lifted Olivia into his arms and carried her to the bedroom, where they tumbled onto the bed in a frenzy of passion and need. Clothes were shed, inhibitions cast aside, as they surrendered themselves to the intoxicating rush of desire.

Their lovemaking was slow and tender at first, a delicate dance of lips and limbs as they explored each other's bodies with reverence and awe. But as their passion grew, so too did their intensity, until they were consumed by a whirlwind of sensation and pleasure.

Griffin lost himself in Olivia, in the softness of her skin, the sweetness of her kisses, the intoxicating scent of her hair. He felt a connection with her that went beyond the physical—a bond that transcended words and logic, binding them together in an unbreakable embrace.

And as they lay tangled together in the aftermath of their lovemaking, Griffin knew that he had found something truly special in Olivia—a love that was as fierce as it was tender, as wild as it was gentle.

In that moment, as they basked in the afterglow of their passion, Griffin felt a sense of peace wash over him—a feeling of completeness that he had never known before. And as he held Olivia in his arms, her heartbeat echoing in sync with his own, he knew that he would never let her go.

A few hours later around 4am Griffins phone vibrated, it was Collins. "Frank, I'm sorry to call at this hour. The fucking Mathematician has left us another body"....

~NINE~

The Calculated Cruelty

Captain Hogan's office was a storm of frustration as Detective Frank Griffin entered, the tension palpable in the air. Hogan's face was flushed with anger, his hands balled into fists as he paced back and forth behind his desk.

"What the shit is going on, Griffin?" Hogan's voice boomed, echoing off the walls of the cramped office. "Another goddamn body, and still no closer to catching this bastard."

Griffin clenched his jaw, feeling the weight of Hogan's words like a physical blow. He knew that the captain's patience was wearing thin—the elusive Mathematician Killer had struck again, leaving another victim in his wake.

"We're doing everything we can, Captain," Griffin replied, his voice strained with emotion. "But this guy... he's like a ghost. He slips through our fingers every damn time."

Hogan let out a frustrated growl, his face reddening with anger. "Well, you better start getting some damn results, Griffin, or so help me God..."

Griffin nodded tightly, his mind already racing with thoughts of the latest murder scene. He knew that time was running out—they needed to catch this killer before he struck again.

As he made his way to the crime scene, Griffin's thoughts drifted to Olivia, the one bright spot in his increasingly dark world. Their relationship had blossomed over the past few months, growing stronger with each passing day. He found solace in her arms, a refuge from the horrors of his job.

But even as he clung to the hope that their love would endure, Griffin couldn't shake the nagging sense of unease that gnawed at the edges of his consciousness. The Mathematician Killer was still out there, still taunting them with his twisted games, and Griffin knew that they were running out of time.

Arriving at the crime scene, Griffin was met with a grim tableau of death and destruction. The victim, a young woman in her early twenties, lay sprawled on the ground, her lifeless eyes staring into the void. Griffin felt a surge of anger and disgust rise within him as he surveyed the scene—the senseless brutality of the murder, the callous disregard for human life.

Beside him stood his partner, Detective Sarah Collins, a sharp-minded investigator with a knack for spotting patterns. Collins met Griffin's gaze with a grim expression, her lips pressed into a thin line as she surveyed the scene before them.

"This is fucked up, Frank," Collins muttered, her voice low and gravelly. "Real fucked up."

Griffin could only nod in agreement, his mind already racing with thoughts of the killer's next move. They had to catch this bastard, no matter what it took.

As they combed through the crime scene for clues and evidence, Griffin couldn't shake the feeling of unease that settled in the pit of his stomach. The killer was playing games with them, toying with their minds and their emotions like a cat with a mouse.

Suddenly, the tension in the air thickened as another pair of detectives arrived on the scene. Griffin's blood ran cold as he recognized the faces of Detective Jake Thompson and his partner, Detective Mike Reynolds. Thompson was a seasoned veteran with a sharp tongue and a volatile temper, and his partner Reynolds was no better—arrogant and abrasive, with a chip on his shoulder the size of Texas.

Thompson's eyes narrowed as they landed on Griffin, a sneer curling his lip. "Well, well, well, if it isn't the golden boy himself," he taunted, his voice dripping with disdain. "Still playing hero, are we?"

Griffin's jaw clenched, his fists tightening at his sides. He had never cared for Thompson, and the feeling was mutual—the two men had clashed on more than one occasion, their animosity simmering just below the surface.

"Save it, Thompson," Griffin growled, his voice low and dangerous. "We've got more important things to worry about than your petty bullshit."

But Thompson wasn't about to back down, his face flushed with anger as he stepped into Griffin's personal space. "You think you're hot shit, don't you, Griffin? Think you can waltz in here and steal my girl?"

Griffin's eyes blazed with fury, his fists clenched at his sides. "Olivia is not your girl, Thompson. She's her own person, and she deserves better than a piece of shit like you."

Before Thompson could respond, Reynolds stepped between them, his voice calm and steady. "That's enough, both of you," he said, his tone brooking no argument. "We're here to solve a murder, not rehash old grievances."

But Thompson wasn't about to let it go, his face twisted with rage as he lunged at Griffin, his fist flying through the air. Griffin ducked and weaved, his instincts kicking in as he fought to defend himself.

The two men exchanged blows, their fists colliding with a sickening thud as they grappled with each other in the dim light of the crime scene. Collins looked on in horror, her hands trembling with fear as she watched the violence unfold before her eyes.

But just as it seemed that things were about to spiral out of control, Reynolds stepped in once more, his strong arms pulling the two men apart. "Enough!" he roared, his voice echoing through the night air. "We need to put our personal shit aside and focus on the task at hand. We need to catch this killer, before he strikes again."

Griffin nodded grimly, his chest heaving with exertion as he tried to catch his breath. He knew that Reynolds was right—they couldn't afford to let their personal vendettas get in the way of their duty. They had a killer to catch, and nothing else mattered.

As the adrenaline faded and the reality of their situation sank in, Griffin felt a sense of determination wash over him. They would catch this bastard, no matter what it took. And when they did, he would make sure that justice was served, once and for all.

And then, just as the first light of dawn began to creep across the sky, a familiar figure emerged from the darkness. It was Professor Einstein, his face drawn and haggard from months of absence.

"I'm back," he announced, his voice tinged with urgency. "And I'm ready to help catch this son of a bitch."

Griffin felt a surge of relief wash over him at the sight of Einstein, a renewed sense of hope coursing through his veins. With the professor back on their side, they stood a fighting chance against the darkness that threatened to engulf them.

But as Griffin looked into Einstein's eyes, he couldn't shake the feeling of unease that settled in the pit of his stomach. The road ahead would be long and treacherous, fraught with danger and uncertainty. But with Olivia by his side and Einstein's expertise at their disposal, Griffin knew that they would face whatever came their way, together.

~TEN~

Unmasking Shadows

Olivia Brooks, the medical examiner for the Boston Police Department, had spent countless hours poring over the details of Jessica Hogan's murder. Though she wasn't the ME at the time of the murder, she had a personal interest in the case—Jessica was the niece of her boyfriend's boss, Captain Joe Hogan. The case was particularly gruesome, and its complexity had kept the department on edge for months.

Jessica's file had been sitting in front of Olivia for hours. The fluorescent lights of her office flickered occasionally, casting a ghostly pallor over the documents. Olivia rubbed her tired eyes and took a deep breath, determined to find something—anything—that the original investigators might have missed.

She flipped through pages of autopsy reports, crime scene photos, and witness statements. Her attention was drawn to the margins of one of the crime scene sketches. There, a series of numbers had been hastily scrawled: 6-1-3-2-5...781. At first, it seemed like gibberish, but Olivia had seen something similar before. It looked like a numeronym, where numbers corresponded to letters.

It took her a while, but finally, the pattern clicked into place. 6-1-3-2-5 corresponded to B-A-D-G-E, and the final three digits, 781, were startlingly familiar. Her heart raced as the realization hit her—781 was Sarah Collins' badge number.

"Oh my god," she whispered, the room spinning around her. "I need to call Frank."

Detective Frank Griffin had seen his share of grim cases, but Jessica Hogan's murder had struck a personal chord. It wasn't just because she was his boss's niece, but the sheer brutality of the crime had left a mark on everyone in the department. When Olivia called him, her voice trembling with urgency, he knew it wasn't good news.

"Frank, you need to come to the lab. Now," Olivia said, trying to keep her voice steady.

"I'll be there in five," Frank replied, hanging up and grabbing his coat.

When he arrived, Olivia was pacing back and forth, the look on her face one of sheer determination mixed with fear.

"What is it, Olivia?" Frank asked, his concern growing.

She handed him the paper with the numeronym. "I found this in Jessica's file. It's a series of numbers that translate to 'BADGE 781'. That's Sarah's badge number, Frank."

Frank's eyes widened as he processed the information. "Are you saying Sarah is involved in this?"

"I don't know," Olivia said, shaking her head. "But it's too specific to be a coincidence. We need to tread lightly. If she's not involved, then she might be in danger. The killer could be targeting her, and if that's the case, it could be because she's close to you."

Frank nodded, the weight of the situation sinking in. "We need to talk to Captain Hogan, but we have to be careful. If the killer is anyone inside the department, this could get very dangerous, very quickly."

They arranged a private meeting with Captain Hogan in his office. The captain listened intently as Olivia explained her findings, his face growing darker with each passing minute.

"You're telling me someone is targeting my niece's case, and they've left a message pointing to Collins?" Hogan asked, his voice a mix of anger and disbelief.

"Yes, sir," Olivia replied. "We need to keep this under wraps for now. If the killer is in the department, we can't trust anyone."

Captain Hogan nodded, his jaw set. "Alright. We'll handle this quietly. Griffin, you and Collins stay on the case, but keep your eyes and ears open. Brooks, I want you to continue going through the files. Find anything that might give us a lead."

Frank and Sarah Collins were partners for years. They had a strong bond, built on trust and countless hours in the field together. Frank couldn't believe she could be involved, but the evidence was undeniable.

"Sarah," Frank began, trying to keep his voice neutral as they sat in their squad car. "I need to ask you something, and it's serious."

Sarah looked at him, her expression one of concern. "What is it, Frank?"

He handed her the note. "Do you recognize these numbers?"

She looked at the paper, her eyes narrowing in concentration. When she saw the final digits, her face went pale. "That's my badge number... What does this mean?"

"We're not sure yet," Frank said, watching her closely. "Olivia found it in Jessica Hogan's case file. We need to figure out why your badge number is there."

Sarah's hands shook slightly as she handed the paper back. "I swear, Frank, I have no idea how this got there. You know me."

"I know, Sarah," Frank said, placing a reassuring hand on her shoulder. "But we need to be careful. If the killer is targeting you, we need to find out why."

As the days passed, Olivia continued to comb through old case files, looking for any patterns or connections that might explain the numeronym. She found a disturbing trend: several old cases, including Jessica's, had small, seemingly insignificant details that pointed to people close to Frank.

There was the case of Tom Jenkins, a small-time drug dealer found dead under suspicious circumstances. In his file, Olivia found another series of numbers that translated to the address of Frank's old partner, who had left the force under mysterious conditions. Another case involved a woman named Lisa Turner, whose case had a note with the initials F.G., Frank's initials.

The realization hit Olivia hard—the killer wasn't just targeting random victims. They were systematically going after people connected to Frank. This was personal.

She needed to tell Frank, but she also needed to protect him. The killer could be anyone, and revealing too much too soon could put them all in even greater danger.

Meanwhile, Frank and Sarah were following up on leads related to Jessica's case. They interviewed old contacts, revisited crime scenes, and dug deeper into Jessica's life. It became increasingly clear that Jessica had uncovered something dangerous before her death.

"She was looking into a series of cold cases," Sarah said, flipping through Jessica's notes. "Cases that were seemingly unrelated, but she thought there was a connection."

Frank nodded, his mind racing. "And now we know there is a connection. But what did she find that got her killed?"

Sarah pointed to a name in Jessica's notes—Professor Albert Wilson , a criminologist who had been consulting on several of the cold cases Jessica was investigating.

"We need to talk to this guy," Frank said. "He might have the answers we're looking for."

Professor Albert Wilson office was a cluttered mess of books, papers, and crime scene photos. He was a tall, thin man with a sharp intellect and a keen eye for detail.

"Detectives, how can I help you?" Wilson asked, looking up from his desk as Frank and Sarah entered.

"We're investigating the murder of Jessica Hogan," Frank began. "She was looking into several cold cases you were consulting on. We believe she might have found something that led to her death."

Wilson's face grew serious. "Jessica was a bright young woman. She was onto something big, but she didn't have all the pieces. I've been continuing her work, trying to connect the dots."

"What did she find?" Sarah asked.

Wilson sighed. "There's a pattern in these cases—a meticulous, methodical approach. The killer is intelligent, careful, and has a deep understanding of forensic science. I've dubbed him 'The Professor' because of the precision of his methods."

Frank and Sarah exchanged a glance. "Do you have any idea who it might be?" Frank asked.

Wilson shook his head. "No, but Jessica was getting close. She mentioned something about a numeronym before she died. It's possible that was the key to identifying the killer."

Frank's mind raced. The numeronym had led them to Sarah's badge number, but it was clear there was more to uncover.

As they left Wilson's office, Frank's phone buzzed. It was a message from Olivia: "Found more connections. Need to meet. Urgent."

Frank and Sarah headed back to the precinct, where Olivia was waiting for them in Captain Hogan's office. She looked exhausted but determined.

"I've been going through more old cases," Olivia said, spreading out a series of files on the table. "The killer has been targeting people connected to you, Frank. This is personal. Look at these cases."

Frank and Sarah examined the files, each one containing a small detail that pointed back to Frank. Addresses, initials, dates—all seemingly insignificant on their own, but together they painted a disturbing picture.

"The killer is systematically going after people in your life," Olivia said. "We need to figure out who it is and why."

Captain Hogan nodded, his expression grim. "We need to tighten our circle. Only a select few can know about this. Griffin, Collins, Brooks—you three are the core team. No one else can be trusted until we know more."

The days that followed were tense. Frank, Sarah, and Olivia worked tirelessly, piecing together the clues left by the killer. They discovered that Jessica had been close to uncovering the identity of the killer before she was murdered. Her notes led them to a series of underground meetings and secret exchanges, each one more dangerous than the last.

One night, while reviewing security footage from a meeting Jessica had attended, Olivia spotted a familiar figure in the background. It was someone who had been around the precinct, someone they had all trusted.

"It's him," Olivia said, pointing to the screen. "That's the killer."

Frank's blood ran cold as he recognized the figure on the screen. It was someone he saw almost every day, someone he had never suspected: Officer Brian Keller. Keller was a quiet, unassuming officer who had been with the precinct for nearly a decade. He was known for his meticulous work ethic and dedication, but Frank had never imagined he could be involved in something like this.

"We need to be very careful with this," Captain Hogan said, breaking the stunned silence. "If Keller is our guy, we can't let him know we're onto him. We need more evidence before we make a move."

Olivia nodded, her eyes still glued to the screen. "I'll go through more footage and see if I can find anything else that links him to the murders. We need to be absolutely sure."

Frank felt a mix of betrayal and determination. "Sarah and I will keep an eye on Keller without raising suspicion. We'll see if he does anything that confirms our suspicions."

The next few days were a tense waiting game. Frank and Sarah kept a close watch on Keller, noting his movements and interactions. They couldn't afford to tip him off, so they maintained their usual routine while subtly gathering information.

Meanwhile, Olivia worked tirelessly, sifting through more evidence and cross-referencing Keller's activities with the known timeline of the murders. She discovered that Keller had been on duty or nearby during several of the murders, but it was all circumstantial. They needed something concrete.

One evening, Olivia found something that made her heart skip a beat. She was reviewing financial records and discovered a series of payments to a consulting criminologist named Dr. James Einhorn. The name wasn't familiar, but the dates of the payments coincided with key points in the investigation. She dug deeper and found that Dr. Einhorn had published several papers on criminology and forensic science under a pseudonym: Professor Albert Wilson

Olivia's mind raced. Could Dr. Einhorn be the link they were missing? She called Frank immediately.

"Frank, I found something. Dr. James Einhorn, also known as Professor Albert Wilson, has been receiving payments that match up with key dates in our investigation. I think he might be involved more deeply than we thought."

Frank's voice was tense. "We'll meet with him again, but this time we'll be more prepared. Keep this to yourself for now. We can't afford to alert Keller."

The next day, Frank and Sarah arranged another meeting with Professor Wilson. They met him in a neutral location, a quiet café away from prying eyes. Wilson greeted them with his usual calm demeanor, but Frank could sense an undercurrent of tension.

"We need to talk about Dr. James Einhorn," Frank began, watching Thompson's reaction closely.

Wilson's eyes widened slightly. "I haven't gone by that name in a long time. How did you find out?"

"It wasn't easy," Sarah said. "We know you've been receiving payments that coincide with key points in our investigation. We need to know why."

Wilson sighed and leaned back in his chair. "I was consulting for the department under the pseudonym to protect my privacy. The payments were for my work on several cold cases. I never intended for my involvement to be secretive, but it appears to have raised suspicion."

Frank nodded, his suspicion not entirely alleviated. "We need you to come to the precinct and help us with this investigation. If you're innocent, your expertise could be invaluable."

Wilson hesitated, then nodded. "I'll do whatever I can to help. Let's get to the bottom of this."

Back at the precinct, Wilson worked closely with Olivia, Frank, and Sarah to analyze the evidence. They discovered more connections between Keller and the murders, but nothing that definitively proved his guilt. They needed a break.

Late one night, as Olivia was reviewing the security footage again, she noticed something she had missed before. In the background of one of the videos, Keller could be seen handing a small package to a shadowy figure. The exchange was quick and furtive, but it was something.

"Frank, Sarah, come look at this," Olivia called out.

They crowded around the monitor, watching the footage. "We need to find out who that other person is," Sarah said. "This could be our break."

Frank nodded. "We'll enhance the footage and see if we can get a clear image of the other person. This might be the evidence we need."

The enhanced footage revealed a partial face, just enough to identify the person: an ex-convict named Leo Marcus, known for his connections to various criminal activities in the city. Frank and Sarah tracked him down to a rundown apartment building on the outskirts of town.

When they confronted Marcus, he was jittery and evasive. "I don't know what you're talking about," he said, his eyes darting around the room.

"We have you on video, Leo," Frank said sternly. "You were seen with Officer Keller. We know you're involved. Tell us what you know, and maybe we can help you."

Marcus hesitated, then sighed. "Alright, alright. Keller hired me to do some jobs for him. Deliveries, mostly. He paid well, and I didn't ask questions."

"What kind of deliveries?" Sarah asked.

Marcus shifted nervously. "Packages. Sometimes money, sometimes... other things. I didn't know what was in them, I swear."

Frank and Sarah exchanged a glance. "We're going to need you to come with us," Frank said. "You're a key witness in this investigation."

With Marcus in custody, they had a potential link to Keller's activities. They continued to build their case, but Keller remained elusive, his actions careful and calculated. They knew they had to act soon before he realized they were onto him.

Captain Hogan called a meeting in his office. "We're getting close, but we need one final push. We need to catch Keller in the act or find undeniable proof of his involvement. Griffin, Collins, I want you to keep pressing Marcus. Brooks, continue your forensic work. We need to wrap this up."

As they left the office, Frank's phone buzzed. It was a message from an unknown number: "Stop investigating or face the consequences."

Frank showed the message to Sarah and Olivia. "Looks like Keller knows we're closing in."

"We can't back down now," Olivia said firmly. "We're too close."

The next few days were a blur of activity. Frank and Sarah intensified their interrogation of Marcus, who eventually cracked and provided more details about Keller's operations. Olivia found additional forensic evidence linking Keller to the crime scenes, but they still needed that one piece of incontrovertible evidence.

One night, while reviewing more footage, Olivia found a clip that showed Keller entering a storage unit late at night. They obtained a warrant and raided the unit, finding a trove of evidence: blood-stained clothing, weapons, and documents linking Keller to the murders.

As they cataloged the evidence, Olivia found a detailed journal outlining each murder, the meticulous planning, and the motives behind them. The final entry chilled her to the bone: "Next target: Sarah Collins."

"We have enough," Olivia said, her voice shaking. "We need to arrest Keller now."

Frank, Sarah, and Captain Hogan, along with a SWAT team, moved quickly. They found Keller at his home, unsuspecting and unaware of the impending raid. The arrest was swift and without incident, but Keller's calm demeanor was unnerving.

In the interrogation room, Keller sat across from Frank and Sarah, his expression unreadable. "Why, Keller?" Frank asked, struggling to keep his emotions in check. "Why did you do it?"

Keller smiled faintly. "You wouldn't understand. It was all a game, a test of intellect and strategy. And you, Griffin, were my final opponent."

Frank felt a surge of anger but kept his composure. "You targeted people close to me, to us. Why Sarah?"

Keller's eyes flicked to Sarah. "Because she was the closest. The final piece of the puzzle. But you were too clever. You caught me before I could finish."

Sarah leaned forward. "You're going away for a long time, Keller. Your game is over."

Keller's smile faded. "Perhaps. But remember, Detective Griffin, there are always more pieces on the board."

With Keller behind bars, the precinct could finally breathe a sigh of relief. But the case had left its mark on everyone involved, especially Frank and Sarah. They knew the scars would take time to heal, but they were determined to move forward.

Olivia, exhausted but relieved, joined Frank at a quiet café to decompress. "We did it," she said, her voice tinged with exhaustion.

"Yeah," Frank agreed, taking her hand. "Thanks to you."

Olivia smiled. "We all did our part. Now, we just have to make sure he stays behind bars."

As they sat together, the weight of the past few weeks began to lift. They knew the road ahead would be challenging, but they also knew they could face it together.

In the days that followed, the department held a press conference, announcing the capture of the serial killer that had terrorized the city. Frank, Sarah, and Olivia stood together, knowing that while the battle was over, the war against crime continued.

And somewhere, in the quiet of his cell, Brian Keller sat, his mind already turning to the next game...

~ELEVEN ~

A New Equation

A month had passed since the arrest of Brian Keller. Life at the precinct had returned to a semblance of normalcy. Frank Griffin and his partner, Sarah Collins, had thrown themselves back into their work, determined to close the chapter on Keller's brutal spree. Frank's relationship with Olivia Brooks, the medical examiner, had grown stronger, their bond solidified by the shared trauma of the investigation.

It was a crisp autumn morning when Frank received the call. A body had been found in an abandoned warehouse on the outskirts of Boston. The details were chillingly familiar, but Frank tried to suppress the rising dread as he and Sarah sped to the scene.

The warehouse was cordoned off with yellow police tape, the cold light of the morning casting long shadows over the crime scene. Olivia was already there, her face pale and serious as she spoke with the forensic team.

"What do we have, Olivia?" Frank asked, stepping under the tape with Sarah close behind.

Olivia looked up, her eyes filled with a mix of sorrow and anger. "The victim is a young woman, early twenties. Cause of death appears to be strangulation, but there are signs of severe trauma and mutilation post-mortem. It's just like the Keller murders, Frank. The precision, the brutality... it's all the same."

Frank's stomach churned. "Keller is behind bars. How could this happen?"

"Come and see this," Olivia said, leading them to the body. She pointed to the victim's arm, where a series of numbers were carved into the flesh: 4-2-6-9-7...314.

Frank stared at the numeronym, his heart sinking. "It's another code," he murmured. "But Keller is locked up. He couldn't have done this."

"Unless he wasn't working alone," Sarah said, her voice tinged with disbelief. "He's got a partner."

Back at the precinct, Frank, Sarah, and Olivia convened in Captain Hogan's office. Hogan's face was ashen as he absorbed the news.

"Keller wasn't working alone," Frank said, his voice tight with frustration. "He's got a partner. The Mathematician Killer."

Hogan's expression darkened. "We thought we had this nightmare behind us, but it looks like we're back to square one. We need to find this partner before more bodies start piling up."

Sarah nodded. "We should start by looking into Keller's contacts, both inside and outside the prison. Maybe there's someone he's been communicating with, someone who's carrying on his work."

"I'll go through Keller's records and see if there's anything we missed," Olivia said. "There has to be something that links him to this new killer."

Frank leaned forward, determination in his eyes. "We need to act fast. If this partner is as meticulous as Keller, they won't stop until we catch them."

Over the next few days, the team delved into Keller's life with renewed vigor. They examined his correspondence, visited his known associates, and scrutinized his activities in prison. Olivia worked tirelessly, combing through forensic evidence and re-examining old case files for any overlooked details.

One evening, as Olivia pored over the crime scene photos from the new murder, she noticed something peculiar. There was a pattern to the numbers carved into the victim's flesh. It wasn't just a random sequence; it was a mathematical series.

"Frank, Sarah, come here," Olivia called out, her eyes wide with realization.

They gathered around her desk as she explained. "These numbers... they're part of a Fibonacci sequence, again. It's a mathematical pattern where each number is the sum of the two preceding ones. This isn't just a code. It's a signature. There are more than one killer but all using different math formulas"

Frank's mind raced. "So, we're dealing with someone who has a deep understanding of mathematics. Someone who's using these sequences to send a message."

"The Mathematician Killer," Sarah murmured. "It fits. But who could it be?"

Frank thought back to their previous investigation, to the clues that had led them to Keller. "What about Professor Wilson? He was consulting on several of the cold cases. He has the expertise, and he knew about the numeronyms."

Olivia frowned. "We brought him in to help us, but he's always been an enigma. We need to take a closer look at him."

The next day, Frank and Sarah visited Professor Wilson at his office. He greeted them with his usual calm demeanor, but there was a hint of wariness in his eyes.

"Detectives, to what do I owe the pleasure?" Wilson asked, gesturing for them to sit.

"We're here about a new murder," Frank said bluntly. "The details are eerily similar to the Keller case. We think Keller had a partner, someone who's continuing his work. We need your help."

Wilson's expression grew serious. "Another murder? That's troubling news. How can I assist?"

"We believe the killer is using mathematical sequences as part of their signature," Sarah explained. "You're one of the few people with the expertise to understand this. Can you take a look at the evidence and see if there's anything we've missed?"

Thompson nodded, his eyes narrowing in thought. "I'd be happy to help. Mathematics can reveal a lot about a person's mind, their patterns and behaviors. Let's see what we can find."

As Wilson reviewed the evidence, Frank and Sarah continued their investigation, following up on leads and questioning Keller's known associates. They discovered that Keller had been corresponding with several individuals outside the prison, including a former student of Wilson's named Evan Blake.

Blake was a brilliant mathematician who had struggled with mental health issues. He had dropped out of Wilson's program several years earlier and had since disappeared from the academic world. Frank and Sarah tracked him down to a small apartment in a rundown neighborhood.

When they arrived, Blake was agitated and defensive. "I don't know anything about any murders," he insisted, pacing the small living room. "I haven't spoken to Keller in years."

"Evan, we just want to ask you a few questions," Frank said, trying to keep his tone calm. "We know you were close to Keller, and we're hoping you can help us understand his methods."

Blake stopped pacing and looked at them with wild eyes. "Keller was a genius, but he was also dangerous. He had this way of manipulating people, getting into their heads. If he's behind this new murder, then you need to stop him. But I swear, I had nothing to do with it."

"Do you know anyone else who might have been working with him?" Sarah asked. "Anyone who shares his obsession with mathematics and murder?"

Blake hesitated, then sighed. "There was one other person... a fellow student named Lydia Chen. She was even more obsessed with mathematical patterns than Keller was. If anyone could be his partner, it's her."

Armed with this new information, Frank and Sarah set out to find Lydia Chen. She had left the university around the same time as Blake and had become a reclusive figure, rarely seen in public. They eventually tracked her down to a small cabin in the woods, a secluded spot far from prying eyes.

As they approached the cabin, Frank's instincts were on high alert. "Stay sharp," he warned Sarah. "We don't know what we're walking into."

They knocked on the door, and after a long pause, it creaked open. Lydia Chen stood in the doorway, her eyes cold and calculating.

Frank took the lead, "Ms Chen, we are with the Boston Homicide unit. Detective Frank Griffin, and this is my partner Detective Sarah Collins"

"We're investigating a series of murders," Frank said, watching her closely. "Murders that involve complex mathematical patterns. We believe you might have information that could help us."

Lydia's expression didn't change. "I don't know anything about any murders. Mathematics is my only obsession."

"Maybe so," Sarah said, "but your name came up during our investigation. We know you were close to Brian Keller."

At the mention of Keller's name, a flicker of something crossed Lydia's face—anger, perhaps, or fear. "Keller was a fool," she said quietly. "He thought he could use mathematics to control the world, but he didn't understand its true power."

Frank stepped closer. "And do you understand that power, Lydia? Do you think you can control the world with your equations?"

Lydia's eyes narrowed. "You have no idea what you're dealing with, Detective. Mathematics is more than just numbers and patterns. It's the language of the universe, and those who can understand it can see the world in ways you can't even imagine."

Frank felt a chill run down his spine. "Lydia, if you know anything about these murders, now is the time to tell us. We can help you, but you need to help us first."

For a moment, Lydia seemed to consider his words. Then she stepped back and closed the door. "Leave me alone," she said through the closed door. "I have nothing more to say."

Frustrated but undeterred, Frank and Sarah returned to the precinct. They shared their findings with Captain Hogan and Olivia, who had been working tirelessly to piece together the puzzle.

"This Lydia Chen sounds like a prime suspect," Hogan said, rubbing his temples. "But without concrete evidence, we can't do much."

"Maybe there's a way to draw her out," Olivia suggested. "If she's as obsessed with mathematics as she seems, we could use that to our advantage."

Frank nodded slowly. "A challenge. Something that will catch her attention and force her to make a move."

Sarah raised an eyebrow. "Like what?"

Frank thought for a moment, then his eyes lit up with an idea. "What if we publish an article in a mathematical journal, something that addresses the killer's patterns and codes? We could hint that we're close to cracking their methods. It might provoke a response."

Olivia nodded thoughtfully. "That could work. If Lydia or any other accomplice is out there, they won't be able to resist correcting us or throwing us off the trail."

Captain Hogan agreed. "It's risky, but it might be our best shot. Let's get to work on it."

Over the next few days, Olivia, Frank, and Sarah collaborated with a mathematics professor from a local university to craft the article. They made sure it contained enough genuine mathematical theory to appear credible while embedding subtle hints about their investigation's progress.

The article was published in a well-respected mathematical journal, and they waited.

A week later, Frank received an encrypted email. It was a response to the article, filled with complex equations and cryptic references that only someone deeply involved in the case would understand. The sender's handle was "Euler's Ghost."

Frank called an emergency meeting with Sarah, Olivia, and Captain Hogan. They gathered in the conference room, the tension palpable.

"We've got a bite," Frank said, displaying the email on the large screen. "Someone calling themselves 'Euler's Ghost' sent this. It's filled with advanced mathematics and veiled threats."

Olivia scrutinized the email. "This is definitely someone who knows their stuff. They're taunting us, but they're also giving us clues. Look at these equations—they reference specific points in time and locations. We need to decode this."

Sarah nodded. "Let's get the cryptographers on it. We need to trace this email and figure out what it's pointing to."

The next few days were a flurry of activity. The cryptographers worked around the clock, deciphering the complex equations and tracking the email's origin. They discovered that it had been sent from a public library in Cambridge, a relatively short drive from Lydia Chen's cabin.

"Looks like we're getting closer," Frank said, feeling a mix of anticipation and anxiety. "We need to stake out that library and see if we can catch 'Euler's Ghost' in the act."

Sarah agreed. "We should also keep a closer eye on Lydia Chen. If she's involved, she might make a move soon."

The stakeout at the library proved fruitful. On the third day, they spotted Lydia Chen entering the building, her demeanor cautious and alert. Frank and Sarah followed her inside, maintaining a discreet distance.

Lydia headed straight for a computer terminal at the back of the library. She logged in and began typing furiously, her eyes darting around nervously. Frank and Sarah moved closer, trying to see what she was doing without drawing attention.

Suddenly, Lydia glanced over her shoulder and saw them. Her eyes widened in panic, and she bolted from the terminal, sprinting towards the exit.

"Go, go, go!" Frank shouted, chasing after her with Sarah right behind him.

Lydia ran through the aisles, knocking over books and patrons in her desperate attempt to escape. Frank and Sarah closed the distance, their adrenaline pumping as they navigated the crowded space.

Just as Lydia reached the front doors, Sarah tackled her to the ground, pinning her arms behind her back. "It's over, Lydia!" she shouted, breathing heavily.

Lydia struggled for a moment before going limp. "You don't understand," she whispered, her voice trembling. "It's bigger than you think."

Back at the precinct, Lydia sat in the interrogation room, her expression defiant yet fearful. Frank and Sarah watched from behind the one-way glass as Captain Hogan entered the room to question her.

"Lydia, we have enough to charge you with accessory to murder," Hogan began, his tone stern but measured. "But we need to know about Keller's partner. Who is 'Euler's Ghost'?"

Lydia remained silent, her eyes fixed on the table in front of her.

Hogan leaned in closer. "We know you're involved, Lydia. The emails, the patterns, it all points to you. Help us, and maybe we can help you."

After a long pause, Lydia looked up, her eyes filled with a mixture of fear and defiance. "You think you've won, but you have no idea what you're dealing with. Keller was just a pawn. The real mastermind is still out there, and they won't stop until their work is complete."

Frank and Sarah exchanged a worried glance. The revelation that Keller was merely a pawn added a new layer of complexity to their investigation. Who was the real mastermind, and what was their ultimate goal?

"We need to dig deeper," Frank said as they left the observation room. "Lydia knows more than she's letting on. We need to find a way to make her talk."

Sarah nodded. "We should also revisit the evidence from Keller's case. If there's a mastermind pulling the strings, there might be clues we missed."

As they poured over the case files once again, Olivia joined them, bringing fresh eyes and insights. They re-examined every piece of evidence, looking for patterns or anomalies that might point to another suspect.

It was during this exhaustive review that Olivia found something peculiar. "Look at this," she said, holding up a piece of paper. "This note was found at one of the crime scenes. It's written in code, but it's different from the others. It uses a more complex cipher."

Frank took the note and studied it. "This could be it. If Keller's partner wrote this, it might give us a lead."

They brought the note to the cryptographers, who worked to decode it. After several tense hours, they had a breakthrough. The note contained coordinates and a date—an abandoned building in Boston, scheduled for demolition in three days.

"This has to be where they're planning their next move," Sarah said. "We need to stake it out and be ready."

The night of the stakeout, Frank, Sarah, and a team of officers positioned themselves around the building, ready for anything. The air was thick with anticipation as they waited for any sign of the mysterious mastermind.

Hours passed, and the night grew colder. Just as they began to worry that it was a false lead, a figure emerged from the shadows, moving stealthily towards the building.

"Hold positions," Frank whispered into his radio. "Let's see what they do."

The figure entered the building, and moments later, another figure appeared. This one was carrying a large bag and moved with a purposeful stride.

"Move in," Frank ordered, leading the charge.

They burst into the building, their flashlights cutting through the darkness. The figures froze, caught in the beams of light. One of them turned to flee, but Frank tackled them to the ground, securing them with handcuffs.

The other figure, cornered by Sarah and the officers, raised their hands in surrender. As they pulled back the hood, Frank's breath caught in his throat.

It was Professor Wilson.

Wilson's expression was one of resigned acceptance as he was led into the interrogation room. Frank and Sarah watched from behind the glass, struggling to comprehend the betrayal.

"I should have seen it," Frank muttered. "He was right there the whole time."

Captain Hogan entered the room, his face grim. "Professor Wilson, you have a lot of explaining to do. Start talking."

Wilson sighed, his shoulders slumping. "You were never supposed to find out. Keller was a necessary sacrifice, a diversion. The true purpose of our work is far greater than you can imagine."

"Enlighten us," Hogan said, his tone icy.

Wilson's eyes glinted with a mix of pride and madness. "Our goal was to understand the deepest secrets of the universe through mathematics. The murders, the codes—they were all part of an experiment to push the boundaries of human understanding."

"And the lives you destroyed?" Hogan demanded. "Were they just collateral damage?"

Wilson looked unrepentant. "Progress requires sacrifice. The knowledge we've gained will change the world."

Hogan leaned forward. "You're going to prison for a long time, Professor. Your 'experiment' ends here."

With Wilson's arrest, the case seemed to reach its conclusion. The mastermind behind Keller's reign of terror was finally caught, and Boston could breathe a sigh of relief.

But for Frank, Sarah, and Olivia, the ordeal had left its mark. They knew the road ahead would be long, filled with challenges and uncertainties. Yet they also knew they could face it together, their bond strengthened by the trials they had overcome.

As they stood outside the precinct, watching the sunrise, Frank took a deep breath. "We did it," he said quietly.

"Yeah," Sarah agreed, a hint of a smile on her lips. "But this is just the beginning, trials and testifying, while still working other cases"

Olivia nodded, her eyes reflecting the dawning light. "We'll face whatever comes next, together."

And with that, they turned to face the future, ready for whatever it might hold.

~TWELVE~

The Return of Einstein

A month had passed since the arrest of Professor Wilson, who had been revealed as a key player in the series of gruesome murders. But even with him behind bars, the sense of unease among the Boston police force remained palpable. The true mastermind was still at large, lurking in the shadows and plotting their next move.

Frank Griffin and his partner, Sarah Collins, had spent countless hours revisiting old case files, scrutinizing every detail for a clue that might lead them to the elusive killer. Frank's relationship with Olivia Brooks, the medical examiner, had grown deeper, their shared determination to solve the case strengthening their bond.

It was on a particularly dreary afternoon when the call came in. Another body had been found, this time in an abandoned building near the harbor. The details were chillingly familiar, sending a cold shiver down Frank's spine as he and Sarah hurried to the scene.

The building was cordoned off with yellow police tape, the usual hustle of the forensic team juxtaposed against the eerie silence of the crime scene. Olivia was already there, her face etched with a mix of frustration and sorrow.

"Olivia, what do we have?" Frank asked, stepping under the tape with Sarah close behind.

Olivia looked up, her eyes betraying her exhaustion. "The victim is a young man, mid-twenties. Cause of death appears to be strangulation, followed by severe mutilation post-mortem. And, just like before, there's a message."

She pointed to the wall, where a series of numbers had been scrawled in blood: 7-6-8-3-9-1-0-2-3. Frank's heart sank. Another numeronym.

Sarah stared at the numbers, her mind racing. "We need to figure out what this one means. It's another taunt."

Frank nodded, his frustration mounting. "We need to bring in someone who can help us decode these faster. Someone who understands the mind behind these numbers."

Sarah's eyes widened in realization. "Professor Wolfgang Einstein. He's the best in his field. If anyone can help us crack these codes, it's him."

Frank hesitated for a moment, then nodded. "Let's get him in. We don't have time to waste."

Professor Wolfgang Einstein arrived at the precinct the next morning, his presence commanding and his eyes sharp with intelligence. Frank and Sarah greeted him, grateful for his assistance yet wary of the complexities ahead.

"Professor Einstein, thank you for coming on such short notice," Frank said, shaking his hand.

Einstein nodded, his expression serious. "I've still been following the case. Have been since we first met, I'll do everything I can to assist."

They led Einstein to the conference room, where Olivia and Captain Hogan were waiting. The numeronym from the latest murder was displayed on the board, a grim reminder of their ongoing battle.

Einstein studied the numbers, his brow furrowing in concentration. "This is no simple code. It's a challenge, designed to taunt you and test your limits. Let's break it down."

As Einstein worked through the numeronym, the team watched with bated breath. Hours passed, and finally, Einstein looked up, a hint of triumph in his eyes.

"It spells out 'You've not got me yet,'" he said, his voice steady. "The killer is mocking you, indicating that they're still out there and watching your every move."

Frank clenched his fists, anger boiling within him. "This has to end. We need to find this person before they strike again."

Einstein nodded. "I'll assist you in any way I can. This killer is clearly a formidable opponent, but they can be caught."

The investigation intensified, with Einstein's expertise guiding their efforts. They delved deeper into Keller and Wilson's backgrounds, searching for any connections that might lead them to the true mastermind. The tension within the team was palpable, each member driven by a relentless desire to bring justice to the victims.

As days turned into weeks, another piece of the puzzle emerged. Olivia, ever vigilant, discovered a pattern in the locations of the murders. Each site corresponded to a point on a geometric shape, a complex design that only someone with a deep understanding of mathematics could create.

"This isn't random," Olivia explained, showing the map to Frank, Sarah, and Einstein. "The killer is following a precise pattern, a mathematical sequence. If we can predict the next point, we might be able to stop them."

Einstein studied the map, his mind racing. "This is brilliant in its complexity. The shape is a fractal, repeating patterns within patterns. If we can determine the underlying formula, we can predict the next location."

Frank felt a glimmer of hope. "Let's get to work. We need to stay one step ahead of this monster."

As the team worked tirelessly to decode the fractal pattern, another murder shook the city. This time, the victim was a young woman, her body found in a park near the university. The numeronym carved into her skin was even more complex, a cruel reminder of the killer's cunning.

Einstein worked alongside Olivia, Frank, and Sarah, his mind a whirlwind of calculations and theories. The pressure was immense, but they were determined to succeed.

After days of intense analysis, Einstein finally cracked the code. "The next point on the pattern is an abandoned warehouse near the river. We need to get there immediately."

Frank rallied the team, and they raced to the location, their hearts pounding with anticipation. The warehouse loomed before them, a silent monolith against the night sky.

They entered cautiously, their flashlights cutting through the darkness. The air was thick with tension, every sound amplified by their heightened senses.

As they moved deeper into the building, they found a hidden room, filled with mathematical equations scrawled on the walls and floors. In the center of the room was a table, and on it, a single piece of paper with another numeronym: 1-4-6-2-5-9-3-8-7.

Einstein studied the numeronym, his face pale. "This one is different. It's a warning."

Frank's heart raced. "What does it say?"

Einstein's eyes were grim. "It says, 'I'm closer than you think.'"

The revelation sent chills down their spines. The killer was not only taunting them but was also confident enough to suggest their proximity. Frank,

Sarah, Olivia, and Einstein knew they had to be more vigilant than ever.

As they regrouped at the precinct, Frank couldn't shake the feeling that they were being watched. The killer's knowledge of their every move was unsettling, and the pressure was mounting.

"We need to find out how they're tracking us," Sarah said, her frustration evident. "There has to be a leak somewhere."

Einstein nodded. "We should sweep for bugs, check for any signs of surveillance. This killer is playing a dangerous game, and we need to turn the tables."

They conducted a thorough sweep of the precinct and their homes, looking for any devices or signs of tampering. It was a painstaking process, but they couldn't afford to leave any stone unturned.

Meanwhile, Olivia continued to analyze the forensic evidence, searching for any clues that might link Keller and Wilson to the real mastermind. The deeper she dug, the more she realized the extent of the killer's manipulation.

"Keller and Wilson were just pawns," Olivia said one evening, her voice filled with conviction. "The real killer is orchestrating everything from behind the scenes, using their knowledge of mathematics to stay one step ahead."

Frank nodded, his jaw set with determination. "We need to find this mastermind and bring them to justice. No more innocent lives should be lost."

The breakthrough came when Sarah discovered a hidden message in one of Wilson's old emails. It contained a reference to a series of lectures given by Professor Wolfgang Einstein at a prestigious conference a few years earlier. The topics included advanced cryptography, mathematical theory, and the psychological implications of numerical patterns.

"This could be it," Sarah said, showing the email to Frank and Olivia. "Einstein's lectures might hold the key to understanding the killer's methods."

They brought the information to Einstein, who was intrigued but cautious. "These lectures covered a wide range of topics, but it's possible the killer attended them and was influenced by the material."

Frank leaned forward, his eyes intense. "Can you identify any attendees who might fit the profile? Anyone who stood out or showed an unusual interest in the subjects?"

Einstein thought for a moment. "There were a few students who were exceptionally keen, but one in particular comes to mind—Dr. Gregory Harlow. He was a brilliant but troubled mathematician who dropped off the radar a few years ago."

With this new lead, Frank and Sarah began searching for Dr. Gregory Harlow. Their investigation revealed that Harlow had been a prodigy, known for his unconventional methods and obsession with mathematical patterns. He had disappeared from the academic world under mysterious circumstances, leaving behind a trail of speculation and intrigue.

They tracked Harlow to a small town on the outskirts of Boston, where he was living under an assumed name. The more they learned about him, the more he seemed to fit the profile of the mastermind they were hunting.

As they prepared to confront Harlow, Frank couldn't shake the feeling that they were walking into a trap. The killer had proven to be incredibly cunning, and they couldn't afford any mistakes.

"We need to be careful," Frank warned. "Harlow is dangerous and unpredictable. We have to approach this with caution."

Sarah nodded. "Let's bring him in and see if he slips up. If he's our guy, we need to catch him red-handed."

They arrived at Harlow's modest house just as dusk settled in, the air thick with tension. Frank and Sarah approached the door, their hands ready to draw their weapons. Frank knocked firmly, and after a few moments, the door creaked open.

Dr. Gregory Harlow stood before them, a man in his late forties with unkempt hair and piercing blue eyes. He looked surprised but not alarmed.

"Dr. Harlow?" Frank asked, his voice steady. "We'd like to ask you a few questions about your research."

Harlow's eyes flickered with curiosity. "Of course, officers. Please, come in."

They followed him into a cluttered living room filled with books, papers, and mathematical models. The atmosphere was suffused with the musty scent of old books and lingering cigarette smoke.

"Dr. Harlow, we're investigating a series of murders connected by complex mathematical patterns," Sarah began, her tone measured. "We've discovered that the methods used resemble some of the theories you've discussed in your lectures."

Harlow's expression remained neutral. "Interesting. I haven't been involved in academia for years. I'm not sure how I can help."

Frank studied Harlow's face, looking for any signs of deception. "We have reason to believe the killer might have attended your lectures and been influenced by your work. Can you think of anyone who might fit that description?"

Harlow's eyes narrowed slightly. "There were many bright minds who attended my lectures. Mathematics attracts a wide range of personalities, some more stable than others. But I can't say anyone stands out as a potential murderer."

Frank pressed on. "What about Professor Wolfgang Einstein? He mentioned you were one of his most promising students."

Harlow's lips curled into a faint smile. "Ah, Wolfgang. A brilliant man. But I haven't been in touch with him for quite some time. Our paths diverged after my departure from the university."

Sarah glanced around the room, her eyes landing on a stack of papers covered in mathematical equations. "These formulas—do they relate to your recent work?"

Harlow followed her gaze and nodded. "Yes, I've been exploring some new theories. Mathematics is a lifelong passion, after all."

Frank's instincts told him Harlow was hiding something, but without concrete evidence, they couldn't make an arrest. They needed more.

Back at the precinct, Frank and Sarah debriefed Captain Hogan and Olivia, sharing their findings and their suspicions about Harlow.

"He's hiding something," Frank said, frustration evident in his voice. "We just need to figure out what."

Olivia suggested a different approach. "What if we use the same tactic we did with the article? We could publish something in a scientific journal, hinting that we're close to uncovering the killer's identity. If Harlow is our guy, he might slip up."

Captain Hogan agreed. "It's worth a shot. Let's coordinate with Einstein and get something published as soon as possible."

The article was published in a prominent mathematics journal, filled with detailed analysis of the numeronyms and the patterns linking the murders. It suggested that the investigators were closing in on the killer, hoping to provoke a reaction.

A week later, they received another cryptic email, this time more threatening in tone. It contained a new numeronym and an encrypted message. Frank, Sarah, Olivia, and Einstein gathered to decode it.

"This one is more complex," Einstein noted, his brow furrowed in concentration. "The killer is escalating."

After hours of intense work, they finally cracked the code. The message read: "Your moves are predictable. You're not as clever as you think."

Determined to turn the tables, Frank and Sarah decided to set a trap. They planted false information suggesting they were planning to move the investigation's headquarters to an old warehouse, hoping to lure the killer into making a mistake.

The night of the operation, they staked out the warehouse with a team of officers, their nerves on edge. Hours passed without any sign of movement, and Frank began to worry that the plan had failed.

Just as dawn approached, they heard the faint sound of footsteps. A figure emerged from the shadows, moving cautiously towards the building. Frank signaled for the team to stay hidden, watching intently.

The figure reached the entrance and began setting up a device. Frank's heart raced. This was their chance.

"Go!" Frank shouted, leading the charge.

They surrounded the figure, weapons drawn. The suspect froze, hands raised in surrender. As they pulled back the hood, Frank's heart sank.

It wasn't Harlow. It was a young man, barely out of his teens, looking terrified and confused.

"Who are you?" Sarah demanded, her voice tense. "What are you doing here?"

The young man stammered, "I-I'm just following orders. Please, don't hurt me."

"Whose orders?" Frank pressed, his frustration mounting.

The young man's eyes darted around in panic. "I don't know his name. He contacted me online, paid me to plant this device. Said it was part of an experiment."

Frank's heart sank further. The real mastermind was still out there, using unsuspecting pawns to do his bidding.

Back at the precinct, they interrogated the young man, but he knew little of value. The killer's web of manipulation was more intricate than they had realized.

"We're dealing with a genius," Einstein said, his voice filled with admiration and dread. "Someone who understands human psychology as well as mathematics."

Frank nodded, his resolve hardening. "We'll catch him. We just need to keep digging."

Days turned into weeks as they continued their investigation. Olivia made a breakthrough when she discovered a link between the victims—each one had attended a lecture or seminar related to advanced mathematics, often featuring Einstein or Harlow.

"This has to be more than a coincidence," Olivia said, showing her findings to Frank and Sarah. "The killer is targeting individuals with a specific background. They're all connected through their interest in mathematics."

Frank felt a surge of determination. "We need to go back to the source. Einstein, can you think of anyone else who fits this profile? Someone who might have felt overshadowed or slighted in the academic world?"

Einstein pondered the question, then his eyes widened in realization. "There was one other student, a prodigy who disappeared under mysterious circumstances. His name was Leopold Fischer."

Fischer had been a brilliant but troubled mathematician, known for his unconventional theories and abrasive personality. He had clashed with many in the academic community, including Einstein.

As they delved into Fischer's past, they uncovered a pattern of erratic behavior and a deep-seated resentment towards those who had overshadowed him. He had the intellect and the motive to be the mastermind behind the murders.

"We need to find Fischer," Frank said, his voice resolute. "He's our best lead."

They tracked Fischer to an abandoned laboratory on the outskirts of the city, a place that had once been a hub of scientific innovation but had fallen into disrepair. As they approached, the tension was palpable.

Frank, Sarah, and a team of officers moved in, their flashlights cutting through the darkness. The air was thick with dust and the scent of decay.

In the main room, they found Fischer, surrounded by a chaotic array of papers and equations. He looked up, his eyes wild and filled with a manic energy.

"Leopold Fischer, you're under arrest," Frank said, his voice steady.

Fischer laughed, a hollow sound that echoed through the room. "You think you've won? You have no idea what you're dealing with."

As they took Fischer into custody, Frank couldn't shake the feeling that the real mastermind was still out there, watching and waiting.

Back at the precinct, they interrogated Fischer, but his answers were cryptic and evasive. He spoke in riddles, referring to a "greater plan" and a "final revelation."

Einstein studied Fischer's notes, his expression growing more concerned. "These equations—they're more advanced than anything I've ever seen. He's working on something beyond our understanding."

Frank felt a chill run down his spine. "We need to figure out what his endgame is before it's too late."

As they continued to unravel Fischer's web of deceit, Olivia made another startling discovery. Hidden among Fischer's papers was a reference to a clandestine group of mathematicians who believed in using their knowledge for radical change. They called themselves "The Order of Pythagoras."

"The Order of Pythagoras," Sarah read aloud, her voice filled with disbelief. "Sounds like something out of a conspiracy theory."

Einstein nodded, his expression grave. "But it's real. These individuals believe they can reshape the world through mathematical principles. Fischer must be a member."

Frank clenched his fists, determination burning in his eyes. "We need to find the rest of them and stop whatever they're planning."

As they prepared for the next phase of their investigation, Frank knew they were closer than ever to uncovering the true mastermind. But the journey was far from over, and the stakes had never been higher.

~THIRTEEN ~

A Mediterranean Interlude

For the first time in months, the precinct was quiet. No new murders, no cryptic codes, no lurking threats. Frank and Olivia decided it was time for a much-needed break. They booked a Mediterranean cruise—ten days exploring the sun-drenched coasts of Greece, Italy, and Spain.

As their ship sailed from port, Frank and Olivia stood on the deck, the salty breeze ruffling their hair. The blue expanse of the Aegean Sea stretched out before them, glittering in the sunlight. They felt the weight of their responsibilities lift, replaced by a sense of adventure and freedom.

Their first stop was Greece. They wandered through the ancient ruins of Athens, marveling at the Parthenon's grandeur. Olivia snapped photos while Frank soaked in the history, his mind temporarily free from the cases that had plagued him. In the evenings, they found secluded spots on the ship's deck, sharing whispered conversations under a blanket of stars. One night, as they watched the moonlight dance on the waves, Frank pulled Olivia close and kissed her deeply, the world around them fading away.

In Santorini, they explored the winding streets of Oia, their hands entwined as they wandered through white-washed buildings with cobalt blue domes. They enjoyed a private dinner on a cliffside terrace, the sunset painting the sky with hues of orange and pink. The evening air was warm, and the sound of the ocean below was hypnotic. Back in their cabin, the tension that had built between them all day finally reached its peak. They made love slowly, savoring each other as if they had all the time in the world.

Next, they docked in Italy. Rome greeted them with its bustling streets and iconic landmarks. They tossed coins into the Trevi Fountain, shared gelato on the Spanish Steps, and lost themselves in the Vatican's awe-inspiring beauty. A sunset walk along the Tiber River, hand in hand, felt like a dream. In Florence, they admired the artistry of Michelangelo's David and strolled through the Uffizi Gallery, each masterpiece leaving them more enchanted. They found a quiet corner in a hidden garden, where Frank kissed Olivia's neck, whispering how much he loved her.

One evening in Tuscany, they attended a local vineyard tour. The rich aroma of aging wine filled the air as they tasted exquisite vintages. Under the golden glow of lanterns, surrounded by the serene beauty of the countryside, they danced to soft music. That night, back in their room, their passion ignited once more. They moved together with a rhythm that felt as timeless as the land they were in.

Spain was their final destination. In Barcelona, they explored Gaudí's fantastical architecture, the Sagrada Família towering above them in its unfinished splendor. The vibrant energy of Las Ramblas pulled them in, and they enjoyed tapas in a lively plaza, their conversations filled with plans for the future. In Seville, they danced to the rhythm of flamenco, the passion of the performance igniting their spirits. The heat of the dance mirrored the fire between them, and back in their hotel, they could barely wait to reach their room before succumbing to their desires.

The cruise concluded with a serene day at sea. Frank and Olivia lounged on the deck, the gentle rocking of the ship soothing their souls. They reflected on their journey, grateful for the time spent together, recharged and ready to face whatever awaited them back home. As the sun set on their final evening, they made love one last time aboard the ship, the gentle lull of the waves matching their rhythm, a perfect end to their idyllic escape.

As they stepped off the plane, reality crashed back in. The precinct was in chaos. Two more young girls had been murdered, their bodies discovered with cryptic codes carved into their skin. The signature was unmistakable—it was the work of the head of The Order of Pythagoras.

Frank's jaw tightened as he reviewed the case files, the familiar sense of dread settling over him. Olivia's eyes were hard with determination. Their respite was over; the nightmare had returned.

Einstein greeted them, his face lined with worry. "We've deciphered parts of the codes, but they're more complex than anything we've seen. It's like they're mocking us, daring us to catch them."

Frank nodded, the fire of resolve burning in his eyes. "We're no closer to an arrest, but we'll find them. We'll stop this."

Olivia squeezed his hand, her expression fierce. "We've come too far to give up now. Let's bring this mastermind down."

Together, they plunged back into the heart of the investigation, their Mediterranean memories a distant, cherished dream. The hunt for the elusive leader of The Order of Pythagoras had never been more urgent, and failure was not an option.

~ FOURTEEN ~

No Closer

Captain Hogan was beside himself. Sitting in his office, you could practically see steam coming off his head. His face was flushed with frustration, his hands clenched into fists on his desk. Griffin and Collins stood before him, waiting for the explosion they knew was coming.

"It's ridiculous, these math clues the mathematician is leaving!" Hogan fumed, slamming his fist on the desk for emphasis. "It's like he's taunting us with something only a damn genius could understand!"

Frank Griffin sighed heavily, rubbing the back of his neck. "I know, for fuck's sake, I'm a high school dropout. Got my GED and joined the force at 20. Math was my worst subject. I'm only a few years from retirement, and I NEED to catch this guy before then."

Collins, with only ten years as a detective, still felt awe every time she stood with Captain Hogan and Griffin. Despite their frustrations, they always impressed her with their dedication and resilience. She learned from them almost daily, their experience shaping her into a better investigator.

Captain Hogan turned his sharp gaze on Griffin. "Frank, the medical examiner is not usually this involved in investigations, but Olivia is proving invaluable. I just don't want her to be in danger, as I'm sure you don't, being involved with her."

Frank's eyes softened at the mention of Olivia. "I don't want her in danger either, Captain. But she's got a knack for this. Her insights have been critical."

Collins nodded in agreement. "Olivia's expertise has given us leads we wouldn't have found otherwise. But we need to find a way to decode these messages faster. Every moment we waste is another moment the killer has to plan his next move."

Hogan leaned back in his chair, his anger momentarily giving way to weary determination. "I understand. But we can't afford any more mistakes. The press is all over us, the public is scared, and the mayor's breathing down my neck. We need results."

Frank clenched his jaw, determination burning in his eyes. "We'll get him, Captain. We'll crack these codes and bring this bastard to justice. We just need to keep pushing."

Hogan gave a curt nod. "Alright. Keep me updated on every development. And Frank, keep Olivia close. We can't afford to lose any more ground on this case."

As they left the office, Frank felt the weight of the captain's words settle on his shoulders. He turned to Collins. "Let's go over the clues again. There has to be something we're missing."

Collins nodded, determination matching his own. "We'll find it. We have to."

Back at the precinct, they pored over the latest set of codes. Frank glanced at Olivia, who was deep in thought, her brow furrowed in concentration. He admired her focus and dedication, but worry gnawed at him. He couldn't shake the fear that the closer they got to the mastermind, the more dangerous the situation would become for her.

"Anything yet?" Frank asked, trying to mask his anxiety.

Olivia looked up, her eyes meeting his. "These codes are more complex than the previous ones. It's like he's escalating, trying to prove something. But I think I'm starting to see a pattern."

Frank's heart quickened with hope. "What kind of pattern?"

Olivia pointed to a series of equations. "These numbers correlate to certain mathematical principles, but they also seem to form coordinates. If

I'm right, they might lead us to his next target or hideout."

Griffin and Collins exchanged glances. "Then we need to follow this lead," Collins said. "It's the best one we've got."

Frank nodded, feeling a surge of determination. "Alright, let's move. We're not letting this bastard stay one step ahead any longer."

As they prepared to set out, Frank took Olivia's hand, squeezing it gently. "Stay close, and be careful."

She nodded, giving him a reassuring smile. "You too, Frank. We'll get through this. Together."

With renewed resolve, the team headed out, ready to confront whatever challenges lay ahead. The hunt for the elusive leader of The Order of Pythagoras was more urgent than ever, and failure was not an option.

~FIFTEEN~

A Family Reunion

Frank Griffin couldn't remember the last time he felt this mixture of excitement and anxiety. His daughters were coming to visit, and it was the first time they would meet Olivia. He wanted everything to be perfect, knowing how important their approval was to him, especially Mary's. Mary, at 36, was only six years younger than Olivia, which made him worry about potential tension.

He spent the morning cleaning his apartment, making sure the spare room was ready for Mary. He even bought a new set of linens, hoping it would make her feel more comfortable. Olivia had offered to help, but Frank insisted on doing it himself. He wanted to show his daughters that he was serious about making this relationship work.

As the afternoon sun began to set, Frank found himself pacing the living room, glancing at the clock every few minutes. Finally, there was a knock on the door. He took a deep breath and opened it, a wide smile spreading across his face as he saw his daughters standing there.

"Hi, Dad!" Mary exclaimed, throwing her arms around him. Sandy and Carol followed, hugging him tightly.

"Hey, girls. It's so good to see you," Frank said, his voice thick with emotion. "Come on in. Make yourselves at home."

The sisters chatted excitedly as they brought in their bags. Sandy and Carol were staying at a nearby hotel, but Mary would be staying with Frank. They marveled at how tidy his apartment was, teasing him about finally learning to clean up after himself.

"Yeah, yeah, very funny," Frank said with a chuckle. "I just wanted everything to be nice for your visit."

They settled into the living room, catching up on each other's lives. Mary talked about her work at the hospital, Sandy shared stories from her latest trip abroad, and Carol regaled them with anecdotes about her kids. As the conversation flowed, Frank felt a sense of contentment. He had missed these moments, the simple joy of being surrounded by his family.

A little while later, there was another knock on the door. Frank's heart skipped a beat. "That must be Olivia," he said, trying to keep his voice steady.

He opened the door to reveal Olivia, looking radiant in a simple yet elegant dress. She smiled warmly, holding a bottle of wine in one hand and a bouquet of flowers in the other.

"Hi, everyone," Olivia said, her eyes bright with anticipation.

"Olivia, these are my daughters," Frank said, introducing them one by one. "Mary, Sandy, Carol—this is Olivia."

Olivia handed the flowers to Sandy and the wine to Carol, then stepped forward to shake hands with Mary. "It's so nice to finally meet you all. Frank has told me so much about you."

Mary's expression was polite but guarded. "It's nice to meet you too, Olivia. We've heard a lot about you as well."

Frank held his breath, hoping the evening would go smoothly. They had reservations at Mary's favorite restaurant in the North End, a charming Italian place that had been a family staple for years.

As they walked to the restaurant, the conversation was a bit stilted, with Frank and Olivia trying to bridge the gap between pleasantries and meaningful discussion. The cobblestone streets and warm, inviting lights of the North End provided a picturesque backdrop, but Frank couldn't help but notice Mary's occasional glances at Olivia.

Upon entering the restaurant, they were greeted by the familiar, comforting aroma of garlic and fresh bread. The hostess led them to a cozy corner table, and they settled in, menus in hand.

Sandy and Carol immediately engaged Olivia in conversation, asking her about her work and interests. Olivia spoke with enthusiasm about her career as a medical examiner, her love of classical music, and her passion for travel. Sandy and Carol seemed genuinely interested, nodding and smiling as Olivia spoke.

Mary, however, remained somewhat reserved. She listened politely but contributed little to the conversation. Frank could feel the tension and decided to steer the discussion towards lighter topics. He shared funny stories from their childhood, and soon the table was filled with laughter.

The waiter arrived to take their orders, and Frank felt a wave of relief. The hardest part seemed to be over. They ordered an array of dishes—bruschetta, calamari, lasagna, and spaghetti carbonara—each one a family favorite.

As they waited for their food, Sandy leaned forward, her eyes twinkling with curiosity. "So, Olivia, how did you and Dad meet?"

Olivia smiled, glancing at Frank. "We met through work, actually. I was brought in to consult on a particularly challenging case, and Frank is leading the investigation. We've spent a lot of late nights working together, and one thing led to another."

Carol grinned. "Sounds like something out of a movie."

Frank chuckled. "Yeah, except with less glamour and more paperwork."

They all laughed, and Frank felt the tension ease a little more. The food arrived, and they dug in, the delicious flavors providing a perfect backdrop for more conversation. Mary started to open up, asking Olivia questions about her family and hobbies. Frank watched with relief as they found common ground.

By the time dessert arrived—tiramisu and cannoli—the atmosphere was warm and relaxed. They shared bites of each other's desserts, laughing and joking like old friends. Frank's heart swelled with happiness. His daughters were getting along with Olivia, and for the first time in a long time, he felt a sense of peace.

After dinner, they walked back to Frank's apartment. Sandy and Carol headed to their hotel, promising to meet up the next day. Mary followed Frank and Olivia upstairs, where they said their goodnights.

As Frank showed Mary to the spare room, she looked around, nodding approvingly. "You've done a good job with this place, Dad. It's nice."

"Thanks, kiddo," Frank said, smiling. "I wanted you to be comfortable."

Later in the evening, Frank and Mary found themselves on the balcony, glasses of wine in hand. The city lights sparkled in the distance, casting a soft glow over them.

Frank took a deep breath, turning to face Mary. "You know you're my little girl, and your opinion matters most."

Mary blushed, looking down at her wine. "You're my favorite dad too," she said with a laugh.

Frank chuckled, feeling a surge of affection for his daughter. "Listen, Mary," he continued, his voice growing serious. "I really love Olivia. It's the first time I've even been close to this feeling since Mom passed. And I think..." He paused, searching for the right words. "I think I want to ask her to marry me, but I need your blessing."

Mary's eyes widened in surprise, but a smile slowly spread across her face. "Oh, Dad, I think that would be lovely. She's great. And with you retiring soon, and your pension, she could retire early and you could have an amazing life together. Mom would want you to be happy. You have my blessing."

Frank felt a wave of relief wash over him. "Thank God," he said, laughing. "And for fuck's sake, can you visit more, please?"

Mary laughed, tears of joy in her eyes. "Yes, Dad, I promise." She leaned in and gave him a big hug, holding him tight. "I'm so happy for you."

They sat in comfortable silence for a while, enjoying the moment. Frank couldn't help but think about the future, about the life he could have with Olivia by his side. For the first time in a long time, he felt a sense of hope.

The next morning, they met Sandy and Carol for breakfast at a charming little café. The sisters continued to bond with Olivia, sharing stories and laughter over coffee and pastries. Frank watched them with a smile, feeling incredibly grateful for the support of his family.

Later, they spent the day exploring the city, visiting museums and parks, and even taking a boat ride on the river. The weather was perfect, the sky a brilliant blue, and the air filled with the sounds of birds and laughter. Frank marveled at how well Olivia fit into their dynamic, how effortlessly she connected with his daughters.

As evening approached, they returned to the apartment. Sandy and Carol headed back to their hotel to pack for their early morning flight. Mary, Frank, and Olivia settled in for a quiet night, enjoying each other's company.

After Mary went to bed, Frank and Olivia found themselves alone in the living room. Frank took her hand, pulling her close. "I have something I want to ask you," he said, his voice trembling slightly.

Olivia looked up at him, her eyes filled with love and curiosity. "What is it, Frank?"

He took a deep breath, reaching into his pocket and pulling out a small velvet box. "Olivia, you mean the world to me. You've brought joy and love back into my life, and I can't imagine spending another day without you by my side. Will you marry me?"

Olivia's eyes filled with tears as she looked at the ring, a beautiful solitaire diamond that sparkled in the light. "Oh, Frank, yes! Yes, I will marry you," she said, her voice choked with emotion.

Frank slipped the ring onto her finger, his heart soaring with happiness. They kissed, a tender and passionate moment that felt like the beginning of a new chapter in their lives.

The next morning, they saw Sandy and Carol off at the airport, promising to stay in touch and visit more often. Mary lingered a bit longer, giving her father one last hug before heading back to her own life.

As Frank and Olivia stood together, watching the plane take off, he felt a sense of completeness.

~SIXTEEN~

New Beginnings

Frank Griffin couldn't contain his elation. Olivia had said yes to his proposal, and although they agreed to marry after catching "The Mathematician," the promise of their future together filled him with renewed determination. The thought of building a life with Olivia, free from the shadows of his relentless pursuit, was a beacon of hope he clung to.

In the following weeks, amidst the chaos of the ongoing investigation, Frank and Olivia began their search for a new home. They decided to keep Frank's apartment in the city for late nights and early mornings, but they would sell Olivia's condo and use the proceeds to buy a house together on the North Shore. With no mortgage on Olivia's condo, they could pay cash for their dream home.

Their weekends were spent driving along the scenic coastline of Swampscott and Marblehead, enchanted by the charm of the seaside towns. The crisp ocean air and the sound of waves crashing against the shore provided a serene contrast to the stress of their work.

The first house they toured was a quaint Victorian with a wrap-around porch and a view of the harbor. Despite its charm, the house felt a bit cramped, and the kitchen, though cozy, lacked the space Olivia dreamed of for their future gatherings.

The second house, a modern colonial, boasted spacious rooms and a large backyard. However, it lacked the character they were looking for, and the view was more of the neighbors' backyards than the scenic ocean they hoped for.

Their third viewing brought them to a stunning three-bedroom, two-bathroom house perched on a slight hill overlooking the Gulf of Maine. The house had a large, open kitchen with floor-to-ceiling windows that offered a breathtaking view of the water. Olivia could already picture herself cooking breakfast while watching the sunrise over the ocean. Frank loved the idea of sipping his morning coffee on the deck, feeling the salty breeze on his face.

As they walked through the house, they both felt a sense of home. The master bedroom had an en-suite bathroom and a cozy reading nook with views of the sea. The other two bedrooms were perfect for guests or a future family. The spacious living room, with its fireplace and large windows, would be ideal for cold winter nights and entertaining friends.

"This is it," Olivia said, her eyes sparkling with excitement. "I can see us here, Frank. This house feels like home."

Frank nodded, pulling her into a hug. "I feel it too. This is where we'll start our new life together."

They made an offer on the house that afternoon, and by the end of the week, it was theirs. Moving in was a whirlwind of packing and unpacking, but every box they emptied and every piece of furniture they arranged brought them closer to their new beginning.

As they settled into their new home, Frank and Olivia found moments of peace and happiness amidst the ongoing investigation. They would spend evenings on the deck, watching the sunset, and planning their future together. But the shadow of "The Mathematician" still loomed over them, and they knew they had to put an end to the madness to fully embrace their new life.

Back at the precinct, the team worked tirelessly, piecing together clues and following leads. Frank's elation from the engagement and the new house gave him a renewed vigor. He and Olivia often stayed late at the city apartment, working side by side, determined to catch the elusive killer.

"We're so close, Olivia," Frank said one evening as they pored over case files. "I can feel it. We just need that one break."

Olivia nodded, her eyes scanning the evidence. "And we will, Frank. We're not giving up."

Their resolve was stronger than ever. With a new home waiting for them and a future full of promise, they knew they had to end the reign of "The Mathematician." Only then could they truly begin their new life together, free from the shadows of fear and uncertainty.

The road ahead was still fraught with challenges, but together, Frank and Olivia were ready to face whatever came their way. With love and determination, they knew they could overcome anything, even the darkest of nightmares.

~SEVENTEEN ~

Unsolved Shadows

Frank and Olivia settled into their new home with a sense of peace and contentment. The large kitchen with its panoramic view of the Gulf of Maine quickly became their favorite spot, and evenings on the deck, watching the sun set over the water, provided a much-needed respite from their grueling work. The house felt like a sanctuary, a place where they could momentarily forget the horrors they faced every day.

But the tranquility of their new life was constantly overshadowed by the grim reality of the unsolved case that loomed over them. "The Mathematician" continued to elude capture, and each passing day without an arrest weighed heavily on Frank's mind.

At the precinct, Captain Hogan gathered the detectives for a crucial announcement. Frank, Olivia, Sarah Collins, and the rest of the team waited in tense silence as Hogan addressed them.

"Listen up, everyone," Hogan began, his voice firm. "We've made some progress, but not enough. This case is getting colder by the day, and we need fresh eyes on it. That's why I've decided to bring in a retired homicide inspector from England. He's a world-renowned expert on serial killers."

A murmur of surprise rippled through the room. Frank exchanged a glance with Sarah, who raised an eyebrow. "Who is he, Captain?" she asked.

"Inspector James Worthington," Hogan replied. "He's consulted on some of the most high-profile serial killer cases in the world. If anyone can help us crack this, it's him."

Frank felt a mix of relief and skepticism. While he appreciated the additional expertise, he knew that no outsider could fully grasp the complexity of the case right away.

A few days later, Inspector Worthington arrived at the precinct. He was a tall, distinguished man in his late fifties, with sharp blue eyes that seemed to take in everything at once. He carried himself with an air of quiet confidence that immediately commanded respect.

"Thank you for coming, Inspector," Hogan said, shaking his hand. "We're grateful for your assistance."

"It's a pleasure to be here, Captain," Worthington replied with a slight British accent. "I've reviewed the case files, and I must say, this 'Mathematician' of yours is quite the enigma."

Frank introduced himself and his partner, Sarah. "Inspector, welcome. We're eager to hear your insights."

"Thank you, Detective Griffin," Worthington said, giving him a firm handshake. "I look forward to working with you all."

As the new task force convened, Worthington wasted no time diving into the details of the case. He brought a fresh perspective, pointing out patterns and anomalies that had previously gone unnoticed. Despite his impressive knowledge and experience, it was clear that this case was unlike any he had encountered before.

Professor Wolfgang Einstein, who had been instrumental in decoding the cryptic messages left by the killer, also joined the task force. His expertise in mathematics and his intimate understanding of the clues added a valuable dimension to their investigation.

Together, the team—Frank, Sarah, Worthington, Einstein, and two other detectives, Jake Thompson and Mike Reynolds—dedicated themselves to unraveling the mystery. They spent long hours examining every piece of evidence, re-interviewing witnesses, and following up on leads.

"These mathematical codes," Einstein mused one evening, staring at a whiteboard filled with symbols, "they're not just messages. They're part of a larger pattern. A sequence that only the killer understands."

"Then we need to understand it too," Worthington said, his eyes narrowing. "We need to think like him. What drives him? What is his ultimate goal?"

Frank leaned back in his chair, rubbing his temples. "We've been at this for nearly 2 years, and we're still no closer. We need a breakthrough, something that ties all these pieces together."

Sarah, ever the optimist, spoke up. "We'll find it, Frank. We just need to keep pushing. There's something we're missing, something that will make it all click."

The task force worked tirelessly, day and night, driven by a shared determination to bring "The Mathematician" to justice. The collaboration between the detectives and the experts fostered a sense of camaraderie, but also a palpable tension as the pressure mounted.

Despite their best efforts, the elusive killer remained one step ahead. Each time they thought they had a lead, it seemed to slip through their fingers. The frustration was palpable, but they refused to give up.

As Frank and Olivia returned to their serene home each night, the contrast between their peaceful domestic life and the horrors of their work became increasingly stark. They found solace in each other's company, drawing strength from their love and the promise of their future together.

One evening, as they sat on the deck, Olivia took Frank's hand. "We'll catch him, Frank. I know we will. And when we do, we can finally put all of this behind us."

Frank nodded, squeezing her hand. "I know. I just hope it's soon. I want to start our life together without this shadow hanging over us."

In the weeks that followed, the task force continued to probe every angle of the case, their determination unwavering. They knew that the key to catching "The Mathematician" was out there, buried in the mountain of evidence. It was only a matter of time before they found it.

And when they did, they would be ready. Ready to end the madness and finally bring peace to their city—and to their own lives.

~EIGHTEEN ~

The Game Unveiled

The partnership between Inspector James Worthington and Professor Wolfgang Einstein proved to be a formidable one. Einstein's unparalleled skill in decoding the cryptic mathematical messages left by "The Mathematician" complemented Worthington's deep understanding of the human psyche and the minds of psychopaths. Together, they dissected each clue, delving into the twisted logic of the killer.

After weeks of relentless work, their combined efforts began to yield results. Patterns emerged from the chaos, subtle connections that had previously been overlooked. The team felt the shift, a growing sense of purpose and direction that had been absent for too long.

One afternoon, Worthington and Einstein called a task force meeting. Frank, Sarah, Captain Hogan, Jake Thompson, and Mike Reynolds gathered in the conference room, anticipation hanging in the air.

Worthington stood at the front of the room, a series of complex charts and notes displayed behind him. "Ladies and gentlemen, after exhaustive analysis, we've uncovered a pattern in the killings. This pattern is intricate, almost elegant in its design, but what stands out is its personal nature."

Einstein stepped forward, pointing to a diagram. "The codes left at each crime scene are not random. They form a sequence that, when decoded, reveals a twisted form of communication. Each message is directed at one person—Detective Frank Griffin."

Frank's eyes widened in shock. "Me?"

"Yes," Worthington confirmed. "The Mathematician is playing a game with you, Frank. In his mind, this is all for fun. He knows you personally, and he's reveling in the chase. Every murder, every clue—it's all part of his sick entertainment."

Sarah looked at Frank, her face pale. "But who could it be? Someone we know? Someone from our past cases?"

Before they could delve deeper, there was a knock on the conference room door. An officer entered, his face grave. "Excuse me, Captain, but The Mathematician struck again. A 21-year-old woman."

The room fell silent as the weight of the officer's words sank in. This latest victim marked the 22nd in two years, all tied to the mastermind of the order. Including the murders committed by Brian Keller, Professor Albert Wilson, Leopold Fischer, and Lars Meier, the total count had reached a staggering 43.

Captain Hogan clenched his fists. "Alright, everyone. Let's move. We need to get to the scene immediately."

Frank felt a familiar surge of determination. The revelations of the meeting had shaken him, but they also fueled his resolve. This had become personal, and he was more determined than ever to bring the killer to justice.

As they prepared to leave, Worthington placed a hand on Frank's shoulder. "Stay focused, Detective. We're getting closer. We will catch him."

Frank nodded, his jaw set in a grim line. "We have to. For all the victims, and for the city. This ends now."

The team hurried out of the precinct, ready to confront the latest atrocity committed by The Mathematician. The road ahead was fraught with danger, but they knew that they were on the verge of a breakthrough. The killer had made this personal, and Frank Griffin was more than ready to rise to the challenge.

~NINETEEN ~

Victim 22

The crime scene was a somber tableau of brutality and twisted artistry. The team arrived to find the street cordoned off, flashing police lights casting eerie shadows on the surrounding buildings. The air was thick with the grim anticipation that always accompanied these cases.

Frank Griffin led the team into the dimly lit apartment, his heart heavy with dread. He braced himself for the horror that awaited them. The stench of blood was unmistakable, mingling with the metallic tang that clung to the air.

The victim lay in the center of the living room, her body meticulously positioned. She was twenty one years old, with long blonde hair that had been carefully brushed and arranged. Her blue eyes stared lifelessly at the ceiling, frozen in a gaze that seemed almost serene if not for the ghastly circumstances.

Captain Hogan was already at the scene, his face etched with anger and sadness. "Her name is Emily Turner," he said quietly, glancing at the body. "She went missing two days ago, and we know she's the 22nd victim of the mastermind of the Order, The Mathematician, because the signature is here."

Olivia knelt beside the body, her gloved hands gently examining the victim's hair and the arrangement of her limbs. "He's getting bolder," she murmured. "The way he's displayed her… it's like he's taunting us."

Frank's eyes shifted to the wall behind Emily. Scrawled in blood was yet another cryptic mathematical message. The symbols and equations were unmistakably The Mathematician's signature, a chilling testament to his twisted intellect.

Sarah Collins took a deep breath, trying to steady her emotions. "She looks so peaceful, like she's just sleeping. But the brutality… it's sickening."

Einstein approached the wall, his eyes scanning the bloody message. "The codes are becoming more complex," he noted, his voice tinged with both awe and disgust. "This one will take some time to decode, but it's clear he's trying to communicate something specific."

Inspector Worthington joined him, his sharp eyes narrowing as he studied the message. "He's accelerating. The intervals between his kills are shortening. He's growing more confident, more daring."

Frank's fists clenched at his sides. "He's not just confident, he's enjoying this. He's treating it like a game, a puzzle for us to solve. And Emily was just another piece to him."

Olivia looked up at Frank, her eyes filled with a mix of empathy and determination. "We'll find him, Frank. We have to."

As the team meticulously processed the scene, they gathered every piece of evidence, every minute detail that might lead them closer to The Mathematician. Emily Turner's life had been brutally cut short, and they owed it to her, and to all the victims, to bring this monster to justice.

Outside, the sky began to darken, the setting sun casting a red hue over the city. Frank stood on the front steps, staring out at the horizon. The weight of the investigation bore down on him, but the promise of a future with Olivia, of peace and normalcy, kept him grounded.

Sarah joined him, her expression grim. "It's not getting any easier, is it?"

Frank shook his head. "No, it's not. But we're closer now than we've ever been. We have to keep pushing. For Emily, and for all the others."

They stood in silence for a moment, the enormity of their task settling over them. But despite the darkness, there was a glimmer of hope. With Worthington and Einstein's insights, and the unyielding dedication of the task force, they had the tools they needed to catch The Mathematician.

As they drove back to the precinct, Frank's mind raced with thoughts of the case and the latest victim. Emily Turner deserved justice, and he was determined to see that she got it. The Mathematician's game was nearing its end, and Frank vowed to be the one to put an end to the madness once and for all.

~TWENTY~

New Developments

The mood in the precinct was one of tense anticipation. Every detective, every officer felt the weight of the investigation bearing down on them. The latest victim, Emily Turner, had left a dark cloud hanging over their efforts. But today, there was a spark of hope.

Captain Hogan called for an urgent meeting in the conference room. Frank, Sarah, Worthington, Einstein, Olivia, Thompson, and Reynolds gathered around the table, their expressions a mix of weariness and determination.

Hogan began without preamble. "We've had a breakthrough. A witness came forward late last night. They saw a man entering Emily Turner's apartment building shortly before we believe the murder occurred."

Frank's eyes widened. "A witness? What did they see?"

"A man in his forties or fifties, light hair, about six feet tall," Hogan reported. "The witness said he didn't recognize him as a resident of the building."

Sarah leaned forward, her voice tinged with excitement. "Did the witness get a good look at his face?"

Hogan shook his head. "Not a detailed look, but it's something. It's more than we've had before."

Olivia cleared her throat, drawing everyone's attention. "That's not all. During the autopsy, I found a hair on Emily's body. It wasn't hers. I've sent it to the lab for DNA analysis."

A collective gasp filled the room. This was the first solid physical evidence they had that could potentially identify the killer.

Frank felt a surge of hope. "DNA could give us a name. This could be the break we've been waiting for."

Worthington nodded thoughtfully. "We need to cross-reference the witness's description with any known associates of Griffin. Remember, The Mathematician has a personal connection to him."

Einstein added, "And once we have the DNA results, we can narrow down our suspects even further. This might be the crucial link we need."

Hogan stood, his expression resolute. "Alright, everyone. Let's get to work. Sarah, follow up with the witness and see if they can remember anything else. Frank, you and Olivia start cross-referencing the description with your personal and professional contacts. Worthington and Einstein, keep analyzing the mathematical patterns. We're closing in on this bastard."

The room buzzed with renewed energy as everyone set to their tasks. Frank and Olivia headed to his office, where they began the painstaking process of going through old case files, looking for anyone who matched the witness's description and had a connection to Frank.

As they worked, Frank glanced at Olivia, grateful for her unwavering support. "We're getting closer, Liv. I can feel it."

She smiled, though her eyes remained serious. "We are. And when we catch him, this nightmare will finally be over."

Hours passed in a blur of files and names. Frank's mind raced as he tried to recall anyone who might fit the profile. His thoughts were interrupted by the buzzing of his phone. It was the lab.

Olivia answered, her face a mask of concentration. "This is Dr. Brooks... Yes... I see. Thank you." She hung up and turned to Frank, her eyes alight with excitement. "They've got a DNA profile. They're running it through the database now."

Frank felt his heart pound in his chest. "How long will it take?"

"Not long," Olivia replied. "We should have a match, or at least a lead, soon."

The minutes ticked by with agonizing slowness. Frank paced the room, his mind racing with possibilities. Finally, Olivia's phone rang again. She answered, her face growing more intense with each passing second.

When she hung up, she turned to Frank, her expression a mixture of triumph and determination. "We have a match. The DNA belongs to a man named Thomas Reed. He has a minor criminal record—breaking and entering, mostly—but nothing violent."

Frank's mind whirled. "Do we know if he has any connection to me?"

"We'll need to dig deeper," Olivia said. "But this is a huge step forward. We have a name, Frank. We have a face."

As they relayed the news to the rest of the task force, the atmosphere in the precinct shifted. There was a palpable sense of momentum, a feeling that they were finally closing in on The Mathematician.

Worthington and Einstein continued to piece together the mathematical patterns, hoping to uncover more about Reed's motives and his connection to the larger scheme. Meanwhile, Sarah and the other detectives worked tirelessly to track down Reed's whereabouts and associates.

The walls were closing in on The Mathematician. Each new piece of evidence brought them closer to ending his reign of terror. And as Frank looked around at his dedicated team, he knew they would see this through to the end.

The killer had made it personal. Now, it was Frank's turn to finish the game.

~TWENTY-ONE~

The First Real Lead

The precinct buzzed with the energy of a new lead, but the elation was tempered by the reality that they were far from catching The Mathematician. The DNA profile had given them a name, but the age discrepancy raised doubts. Frank Griffin and his partner, Sarah Collins, were determined to follow every lead, no matter how tenuous.

Frank and Olivia were huddled together in his office, reviewing the latest information. Frank's frustration was palpable. "So, the DNA matches Thomas Reed, but the witness saw a man in his forties. What the hell does that mean?"

Olivia sighed, rubbing her temples. "It means we're not out of the woods yet. The hair could have been transferred from her clothing. Reed could be innocent, but we can't rule him out until we talk to him."

"Damn it," Frank muttered. "We're so close, Liv. I can feel it."

Olivia reached out, her hand finding his. "We'll get there, Frank. We just have to keep pushing."

Frank leaned in and kissed her deeply, their connection electric. The kiss was long and passionate, the kind that could easily lead to more if they had the time. But duty called, and they both knew it. As they pulled away, their eyes locked with a promise of more to come.

"I love you," Frank said, his voice husky with emotion.

"I love you too," Olivia replied, a soft smile playing on her lips.

With a final kiss, Frank left Olivia's office and found Sarah Collins. "Let's go, Sarah. We need to talk to Reed."

They drove across town to Thomas Reed's apartment, a swanky high-rise in an upscale neighborhood. Reed was a social media influencer, living a life of luxury funded by his vast online following. When they arrived, the doorman directed them to the 20th floor.

Reed's apartment was as ostentatious as they had expected—modern furnishings, floor-to-ceiling windows with a panoramic view of the city, and a palpable air of wealth. Reed himself answered the door, his red hair perfectly styled, his demeanor annoyingly smug.

"Detectives," he greeted them with a cocky grin. "What can I do for you?"

Frank and Sarah exchanged glances, both immediately put off by Reed's attitude. "We need to ask you some questions about Emily Turner," Frank said, his tone all business.

Reed's grin faltered slightly, but he quickly recovered. "Emily? What about her? We broke up a month ago."

Frank held up a photo of Emily. "When was the last time you saw her?"

Reed shrugged, leaning casually against the doorframe. "About a month ago, like I said. We had a fight, and that was it."

Sarah stepped forward, her eyes narrowing. "A witness saw someone matching your description entering Emily's apartment building the night she was killed."

Reed's eyes widened briefly before he masked his surprise with a smirk. "Wasn't me. I've got alibis for that night. You can check my social media—lots of live streams, plenty of witnesses."

Frank's patience was wearing thin. "Mind if we take a look around your apartment?"

Reed's smirk disappeared. "Do you have a warrant?"

"We can get one," Frank replied, his voice hard.

Reed sighed dramatically. "Fine. Look around. You won't find anything."

As Frank and Sarah searched the apartment, they found nothing that tied Reed directly to the crime. No blood, no incriminating evidence—nothing. Reed watched them with an air of boredom, his confidence unshaken.

After an exhaustive search, they had to admit defeat. Frank turned to Reed, his frustration barely contained. "We'll be in touch, Reed. Don't leave town."

Reed flashed a triumphant smile. "Wouldn't dream of it, Detective."

Back in the car, Frank slammed his fist against the steering wheel. "Damn it! We're back to square one."

Sarah tried to stay optimistic. "At least we ruled him out. That's something."

"Yeah," Frank muttered. "But it's not enough."

As they drove back to the precinct, Frank's mind raced. They were running out of time, and The

Mathematician was still out there, planning his next move. But with every dead end, Frank's resolve only grew stronger. They would catch this killer, no matter what it took.

~TWENTY-TWO-

Getting Closer

The precinct was a flurry of activity as Frank and Sarah returned from their interview with Thomas Reed. Despite ruling him out as a suspect, they were no closer to catching The Mathematician. But hope arrived in the form of Emily Turner's computer.

Olivia and a team of forensic analysts had been meticulously going through Emily's digital life. It was Olivia who found the breakthrough. She called Frank and Sarah into the tech lab, where her face was lit by the glow of multiple monitors.

"Frank, Sarah, we found something," Olivia said, her voice a mixture of excitement and caution. "Emily was in contact with members of The Order."

Frank's eyes widened. "What did you find?"

Olivia gestured to one of the screens. "Emily's computer has a chat history with several members of The Order. Most of the conversations are encrypted, but we managed to decrypt some parts. There's a lot of talk about their leader, who they refer to as 'The Architect.' It's clear this person is in academia, but they never mention a name."

Sarah leaned over to read the messages. "This is huge. Can we trace any of the chat participants?"

Olivia nodded. "We traced the IP addresses to a few locations. Two of them are local: a Dr. Peter Marlow, a mathematics professor at MIT, and Lisa Novak, a postgraduate student at Harvard."

Frank felt a surge of determination. "Let's bring them in for questioning. If they're part of The Order, they might know something that can lead us to The Mathematician."

Interview with Dr. Peter Marlow

Dr. Peter Marlow's office was a cluttered mess of books, papers, and mathematical models. He was a middle-aged man with thinning hair and a nervous demeanor. Frank and Sarah sat across from him, their expressions stern.

"Dr. Marlow, we're investigating the murder of Emily Turner," Frank began. "We have evidence that links her to an online group known as The Order. Your IP address was identified as one of the participants in these chats."

Marlow's face paled. "I-I don't know anything about any murder. Yes, I participated in those chats, but it was all theoretical. We discussed mathematical principles, nothing more."

Sarah leaned forward, her voice calm but firm. "We need to know about The Architect. Who is he?"

Marlow swallowed hard. "I've never met him in person. He's a brilliant mathematician, but very secretive. We only communicated through encrypted messages. He's in academia, like most of us, but I don't know his real identity."

Frank sighed, frustration bubbling under the surface. "Did Emily ever mention meeting The Architect or any of the other members in person?"

Marlow shook his head vigorously. "No, she was just as curious as the rest of us. She admired his work but was frustrated by the lack of personal interaction."

Interview with Lisa Novak

Lisa Novak's apartment was a stark contrast to Marlow's cluttered office. It was minimalist, almost clinical, with nothing out of place. She was a sharp, confident woman in her early twenties, her eyes bright with intelligence.

"Ms. Novak, we're here about Emily Turner," Sarah started. "We know you were in contact with her through The Order. What can you tell us about your interactions?"

Lisa didn't flinch. "Emily and I talked a lot about mathematics and The Order's principles. We were both fascinated by the idea of applying mathematical theory to real-world problems. But we never discussed anything illegal."

Frank cut in, his voice intense. "What about The Architect? Did you ever meet him or know his real identity?"

Lisa's eyes narrowed. "No one knows who he is. He's extremely careful. We only ever communicated online. I did get the impression that he's someone with a significant position in the academic world. But that's it."

Sarah pressed on. "Did Emily ever express any fears or concerns about her involvement with The Order?"

Lisa hesitated, then nodded slowly. "She did, actually. A few weeks before she died, she mentioned feeling like she was being watched. She thought it might be The Architect, or someone close to him. But she didn't have any proof, and she didn't want to stop her research."

Frank and Sarah exchanged a glance. This was more than they had before, but it still wasn't enough.

Back at the precinct, Frank, Sarah, Olivia, Worthington, and Einstein gathered to review the new information. They pored over the chat logs, the interviews, and the profiles of Marlow and Novak.

"It's clear that The Architect is playing a very careful game," Worthington mused. "He's manipulating these individuals, using their brilliance for his own ends. We need to find a way to draw him out."

Einstein nodded, his expression thoughtful. "The key might be in the mathematical patterns themselves. If we can crack his code, we might find something he overlooked."

Olivia added, "And we should keep a close eye on Marlow and Novak. If they're part of The Order, they might inadvertently lead us to The Architect."

Frank felt a flicker of hope. They were closer than ever, but the final piece of the puzzle was still missing. They had to stay vigilant, keep pressing, and never let their guard down. The Mathematician's game was far from over, but they were closing in on him, step by step.

As the team continued their work, Frank couldn't help but feel a renewed sense of purpose. They were getting closer. And soon, The Mathematician would slip up, and when he did, they would be ready.

~TWENTY-THREE~

Following the Leads

The investigation pressed on with a relentless intensity as Frank, Sarah, and the rest of the team pursued every lead, leaving no stone unturned in their quest to catch The Mathematician. The precinct hummed with activity, the air thick with anticipation and tension.

Frank and Sarah spent countless hours poring over evidence, interviewing potential witnesses, and combing through databases for any hint of The Architect's identity. Meanwhile, Olivia and her team worked tirelessly in the lab, analyzing DNA samples, digital evidence, and forensic traces left at the crime scenes.

Every lead, no matter how small, was followed with meticulous precision. They tracked down associates of The Order, cross-referenced chat logs, and conducted surveillance on anyone remotely connected to the case. The pressure was relentless, but they refused to relent in their pursuit of justice.

Despite their efforts, the elusive mastermind remained one step ahead, leaving them with more questions than answers. But with each new piece of information, they felt themselves inching closer to the truth.

They followed a trail of breadcrumbs through the seedy underbelly of the city, delving into the shadows where The Mathematician lurked. They encountered a web of deception and deceit, encountering suspects who ranged from petty criminals to high-ranking academics.

They visited seedy bars and rundown apartments, searching for any clue that might lead them to The Architect. They interrogated suspects, their words dripping with lies and half-truths, but they refused to be deterred.

As the days turned into weeks, the pressure mounted, each dead end driving them to push harder, to dig deeper into the darkness that surrounded them. They worked tirelessly, fueled by a relentless determination to bring The Mathematician to justice.

And then, as they thought they were making progress, tragedy struck. Sarah Collins received a call, her face paling as she listened to the voice on the other end. When she hung up, her expression was grim.

"Frank," she said, her voice barely above a whisper, "you won't believe this, but Lisa Novak's body has just been found in an abandoned warehouse near the airport."

Frank felt a chill run down his spine as the weight of the news settled over him. Lisa Novak, another victim of The Mathematician's twisted game. They had failed to protect her, failed to stop the killer before he struck again.

But amidst the despair, there was a flicker of determination in Frank's eyes. They were getting closer. With each new piece of evidence, each new lead, they were narrowing the gap between them and The Mathematician. And they would not rest until he was brought to justice, no matter the cost.

~TWENTY-FOUR~

The Murder Scene

The abandoned warehouse loomed in the darkness, its once-grand facade now a crumbling monument to decay. Frank Griffin and his team approached cautiously, their flashlights cutting through the shadows as they navigated the desolate interior.

The scene was eerily familiar, yet chillingly different. Lisa Novak's lifeless body lay sprawled on the cold concrete floor, her brown hair matted with blood. The air was heavy with the stench of death, and Frank felt a knot tighten in his stomach as he surveyed the grim tableau before him.

But it was the message scrawled in bold red chalk that sent a shiver down Frank's spine. Unlike the cryptic clues left at previous crime scenes, this message was chillingly direct:

"Math is my passion, but murder is fun. Look, Frankie, I've got you on the run.
Los, fang mich."

Frank's blood ran cold as he read the words. The taunting, mocking tone was unmistakable, and he felt a surge of anger boiling within him.

"What the shit?" Hogan exclaimed, his usually composed demeanor shattered by the gruesome sight before him. "Now he's a fucking poet? And what the hell is 'Los fang mich'?"

Frank's jaw clenched as he struggled to contain his rage. "I'm getting really pissed," he muttered through gritted teeth. "This son of a bitch has it in for me."

Thompson stepped forward, his brow furrowed in concentration. "It looks like German, but I'm not sure what it means. Mike, let's head over to the university and ask Professor Einstein if he knows."
"Hold on I'll come with you", said Griffin. "Sarah go back and work more with Olivia, I'll meet up with you guys later"

At the university, Griffin, Reynolds and Thompson, found Professor Einstein in his office, surrounded by books and papers. The renowned mathematician greeted them warmly, his expression serious as they explained the situation.

"Los fang mich," Thomas repeated, his voice tight with frustration. "Do you know what it means?"

Einstein's brow furrowed as he considered the words. "'Los' is German for 'let's' or 'come on.' And 'fang mich' means 'catch me.' It's a taunt, a challenge."

Frank's fists clenched at his sides. "So he's daring me to catch him."

Einstein nodded gravely. "It would seem so. The Mathematician is playing a dangerous game, Frank. He's toying with you, testing your limits."

Thompson frowned, his mind racing with possibilities. "But why German? What's the significance?"

Einstein shrugged. "It's hard to say. Perhaps it's a clue to his identity, or maybe he's just trying to throw us off track. Either way, we need to tread carefully."

As they left the university, Frank's thoughts were consumed by the chilling message left by The Mathematician. The killer's taunts only fueled his determination to bring him to justice, no matter the cost.

But as they returned to the precinct, Frank couldn't shake the feeling that The Mathematician was always one step ahead, always watching, waiting for the perfect moment to strike again.
And with each passing day, the stakes grew higher, the danger more real than ever before.

~TWENTY-FIVE~

The Cat and Mouse Game

The taunting message left by The Mathematician haunted Frank Griffin like a dark shadow, a constant reminder of the killer's twisted game. As the investigation pressed on, Frank couldn't shake the feeling that The Mathematician was deliberately leaving clues, almost as if he wanted to be caught.

The precinct buzzed with activity as Frank and his team poured over every detail of the case, dissecting the message and searching for any hidden meanings. The atmosphere was tense, the pressure mounting with each passing day as they raced against time to catch the elusive killer.

But despite their best efforts, The Mathematician remained one step ahead, his true identity still shrouded in mystery. Frank felt a growing sense of frustration and desperation, the weight of the case bearing down on him like a heavy burden.

As they followed every lead and chased down every clue, Frank couldn't help but feel like they were playing a dangerous game of cat and mouse with The Mathematician. The killer seemed to revel in the chase, leaving breadcrumbs for them to follow, taunting them with his cryptic messages and twisted poetry.

But Frank refused to be intimidated. He knew that The Mathematician's arrogance would be his downfall, that eventually he would make a mistake and they would be there to catch him. And so, with dogged determination, Frank and his team pressed on, determined to bring the killer to justice and end his reign of terror once and for all.

As they delved deeper into the darkness that surrounded them, Frank couldn't help but wonder what drove The Mathematician to commit such heinous acts. Was it a thirst for power? A desire for control? Or was it something darker, something beyond comprehension?

But as the days turned into weeks and the investigation seemed to stall, Frank knew that they were running out of time. The Mathematician was out there, watching and waiting, his next move already planned. And if they didn't catch him soon, the consequences would be catastrophic.

But Frank refused to give up hope. He knew that as long as they stayed one step ahead, as long as they remained vigilant and focused, they would eventually catch The Mathematician and bring him to justice. And so, with renewed determination, Frank and his team continued their relentless pursuit, knowing that the fate of countless lives hung in the balance.

~TWENTY-SIX~

The German Message

"There's something really strange about this German message left at the scene," thought Griffin, staring at the chalked words on the evidence board. "But why? Why leave us a message like that? Directed at me, nonetheless."

Frank's mind raced as he tried to unravel the significance behind The Mathematician's latest taunt. The killer's decision to use German seemed calculated, a deliberate attempt to convey something deeper. But what?

He gathered the team in the conference room. "Alright, everyone," Frank began, "I need your thoughts on this German message. 'Los, fang mich'—'come on, catch me.' Why German? What's the connection?"

Collins leaned back in her chair, her brow furrowed in thought. "It could be a red herring, something to throw us off track. Or maybe it's a clue to his identity."

Worthington, the retired homicide inspector from England, chimed in. "Serial killers often have patterns or obsessions. The German could be linked to his background or something that holds significance for him. It might not be random."

Einstein nodded in agreement. "We need to consider his profile. The Mathematician is meticulous, methodical. The use of German suggests a certain level of education, perhaps even a specific cultural or academic connection."

Frank stared at the board, his eyes narrowing. "Let's start digging into his past victims again, focusing on any potential German connections—whether it's through their backgrounds, places they frequented, or people they associated with."

The team split up, each taking a segment of the case to reexamine. Collins and Worthington sifted through old files, searching for any German ties in the victims' histories. Frank and Olivia revisited the forensic evidence, looking for patterns that might have been previously overlooked.

Hours turned into days as they painstakingly combed through records and re-interviewed witnesses. The investigation led them to German-language classes at local universities, cultural events, and even German-speaking communities within the city. Each clue seemed to inch them closer, yet the identity of The Mathematician remained frustratingly out of reach.

One afternoon, Collins burst into Frank's office, excitement lighting up her face. "Frank, I think I've found something. One of the victims, Julia Krauss, was enrolled in a German literature course at the university. The professor, Dr. Werner Schmidt, is a prominent figure in German studies."

Frank's heart raced. "Good work, Sarah. Let's go talk to Dr. Schmidt and see if he knows anything that could help us."

Dr. Werner Schmidt's office was lined with bookshelves, each crammed with volumes of German literature and cultural studies. The professor greeted them warmly, though his eyes were shadowed with worry as he learned of their purpose.

"I remember Julia Krauss well," Dr. Schmidt said, his voice tinged with sadness. "She was one of my brightest students. It's tragic what happened to her."

Frank got straight to the point. "Professor, we found a message in German at the latest crime scene. 'Los, fang mich.' Do you have any idea why the killer might use German?"

Schmidt's brow furrowed in thought. "German is a language of precision and logic, much like mathematics. It's possible the killer has an academic background that intersects with both fields. He might be trying to communicate something specific, or he could be taunting you with his knowledge."

Frank nodded, absorbing the information. "Is there anyone in your department or in the academic community who fits the profile? Someone with a deep knowledge of both mathematics and German culture?"

Dr. Schmidt hesitated, clearly reluctant to cast suspicion. "There are a few individuals who come to mind, but I can't say for certain without more information. I'll compile a list for you."

Back at the precinct, the team pored over the list of names provided by Dr. Schmidt. Each person was scrutinized, their backgrounds checked for any signs of a connection to the murders. The investigation was grueling, but they were getting closer.

Frank felt a glimmer of hope. They were narrowing down the possibilities, tightening the net around The Mathematician. But with each step forward, the danger escalated, and the killer's taunts grew more personal.

As the team continued their relentless pursuit, Frank couldn't shake the feeling that they were on the brink of a breakthrough. The German message was a key piece of the puzzle, and he was determined to decipher it before the killer struck again.

But even as they closed in, The Mathematician watched from the shadows, his twisted game far from over.

~TWENTY-SEVEN~

The Shortlist

Dr. Werner Schmidt was true to his word. Within a day, he had compiled a list of six names—individuals with a deep knowledge of both mathematics and German culture. Frank and his team gathered in the conference room to review the list.

"Alright," Frank began, "let's go through these names one by one."

Sarah Collins read the first name aloud. "Dr. Helmut Richter. He passed away two years ago from a heart attack."

"Cross him off," Frank said, feeling a pang of disappointment. "Next?"

"Professor Heinrich von Deusen
Died at 38 in a fiery car crash"

"Next" said Griffin

"Annalise Bauer," Collins continued, "she moved back to Germany a few years ago. We'll still check into her background, but it's unlikely she's our killer."

"Agreed," Worthington chimed in. "Let's focus on the ones still within our reach."

"Dr. Klaus Meyer," Collins read, "he's currently a professor in California."

Frank nodded. "We'll reach out to the local authorities there and have them follow up. But for now, let's concentrate on those closer to home."

Collins scanned the list again. "That leaves two: Dr. Karl Zimmerman and Dr. Martin Weber, both still residing in Massachusetts."

Frank felt a spark of hope. "Alright, let's divide and conquer. Sarah, you and I will take Dr. Zimmerman. Worthington, you and Thompson can handle Dr. Weber. Let's see if we can shake something loose."

Frank and Collins drove to Cambridge, where Dr. Karl Zimmerman lived in a modest, well-kept house near the university. The professor welcomed them inside, his demeanor calm but curious.

"Dr. Zimmerman," Frank began, "we're investigating a series of murders connected to The Mathematician.

We have reason to believe the killer might have a background in both mathematics and German culture. Can you tell us about your work and if you've noticed anything unusual among your colleagues?"

Zimmerman's eyes widened in shock. "Murders? That's horrifying. I've spent most of my career studying mathematical theories and teaching. I can't think of anyone who would be capable of such atrocities. But I'll help in any way I can."

Frank and Collins spent the next hour questioning Zimmerman, but his answers provided no new leads. Despite his cooperation, they left his home feeling frustrated and no closer to finding their suspect.

Meanwhile, Worthington and Thompson were in the picturesque town of Salem, visiting Dr. Martin Weber. Weber's house was filled with books and scholarly articles, a testament to his academic pursuits.

"We're investigating The Mathematician," Worthington explained after introductions. "We've found a message in German at the latest crime scene. Do you know anyone in your field who might be connected to these crimes?"

Weber looked genuinely distressed. "I've heard about the murders, of course, but I can't imagine anyone in our community being involved. My work is purely theoretical. Mathematics and German literature have always been passions of mine, but to think someone could twist that knowledge for such evil... it's unthinkable."

They probed further, asking about Weber's colleagues and any unusual behavior he might have noticed. Weber offered a few names of people he'd worked with over the years but insisted he couldn't imagine any of them committing such crimes.

As Worthington and Thompson wrapped up their interview, they exchanged a look of mutual frustration. Like Zimmerman, Weber appeared to be nothing more than a dedicated academic, far removed from the violent world of The Mathematician.

Back at the precinct, the team reconvened to share their findings. The frustration in the room was palpable.

"Zimmerman and Weber both seem clean," Frank said, running a hand through his hair. "We're back to square one."

"We need to keep digging," Worthington urged. "The Mathematician has made a mistake before, and he'll make one again. We just have to be ready."

Olivia, who had been quietly examining the case files, suddenly spoke up. "There's something I've been thinking about. The German message—it's not just a taunt. It's a clue. He wants us to find him, but only on his terms."

"What do you mean?" Frank asked, intrigued.

"Think about it," Olivia continued. "He's playing a game. He's challenging you, Frank. The German message is part of that game, a breadcrumb leading us closer. We need to look at it from his perspective, figure out what he wants us to see."

Frank nodded slowly, the pieces of the puzzle starting to come together in his mind. "You're right. He's not just taunting us—he's guiding us. We need to follow the clues, but we also need to be ready for anything. He's unpredictable, and he's dangerous."

The team redoubled their efforts, pouring over the evidence with renewed determination. They knew they were getting closer, inching ever nearer to unmasking The Mathematician. But the stakes were higher than ever, and the killer's next move could come at any moment.

Frank felt the weight of the responsibility on his shoulders, but he was more determined than ever to catch The Mathematician and put an end to his deadly game once and for all.

~TWENTY-EIGHT-

Digging Deeper

Frank Griffin sat at the head of the table in the precinct's conference room, the air heavy with tension. The interviews with Dr. Karl Zimmerman and Dr. Martin Weber had turned up nothing useful, and the sense of frustration was palpable. They needed a breakthrough, and they needed it fast.

"Alright," Frank began, looking around at his team. "Since Zimmerman and Weber are off the list, let's look into the others. We can't afford to leave any stone unturned."

Sarah Collins nodded, flipping through her notes. "We've got Professor Heinrich von Deusen next. Died at 38 in a fiery car crash."

Frank rubbed his chin thoughtfully. "A car crash can be staged. Let's dig into his background. If he was our guy, there might be something that links him to these murders."

They split up the tasks, and Collins was assigned to dig deeper into von Deusen's past. She started with public records, tracking down any significant events in his life. What she found was a dark and disturbing history.

Later that afternoon, Collins reported back to the team with her findings. "Professor Heinrich von Deusen had a seriously messed-up life. I managed to get in touch with his former psychiatrist, Dr. Alice Morgan. She was willing to talk, under the condition of anonymity."

"What did she say?" Frank asked, leaning forward.

"Von Deusen had a traumatic childhood. According to Dr. Morgan, he was molested by his young mother. This kind of trauma often leads to severe psychological issues. And it gets worse—he had a habit of mutilating small animals as a child."

Worthington winced. "Classic signs of a developing psychopath."

Collins continued, "He was arrested twice for rape in his twenties, but the cases were dismissed due to technicalities. Dr. Morgan believes he was a ticking time bomb."

"Jesus," Frank muttered. "He fits the profile, but if he died in that car crash, how could he be our guy?"

"Maybe he didn't die," Olivia suggested. "Maybe he faked his death and continued his twisted activities under a new identity."

"That's a possibility," Worthington agreed. "We should confirm his death. If there's any doubt, we need to follow up."

The next day, Frank and Collins visited the site of von Deusen's supposed death. The car crash had occurred on a lonely stretch of road, and the investigation at the time had been brief, chalking it up to an accident.

They met with the local coroner who had handled the case, Dr. Bernard Fletcher. "Can you confirm that von Deusen's body was positively identified?" Frank asked.

Dr. Fletcher scratched his head. "Well, the body was badly burned. Dental records were used for identification, but there's always a margin for error."

"Is there any chance he could have staged his death?" Collins pressed.

Fletcher looked thoughtful. "It's not impossible, but it would have been difficult. The crash was quite severe."

"We need to be sure," Frank insisted. "Could we exume the body and run a DNA test?"

Fletcher hesitated, then nodded. "I'll make the necessary arrangements, but it'll take some time."

While they waited for the results, the team continued to investigate von Deusen's life. They tracked down former colleagues and students, piecing together a picture of a deeply troubled man. The more they learned, the more they became convinced that von Deusen could very well be their killer.

A week passed, the DNA results came in. Dr. Fletcher called Frank with the news. "The DNA from the exhumed body doesn't match von Deusen's. Whoever died in that car crash, it wasn't him."

Frank felt a chill run down his spine. "So he's still out there. Living under a new identity, continuing his killing spree."

Collins looked determined. "We need to find out who he became. Someone like that wouldn't just disappear quietly. There has to be a trail."

Worthington nodded. "We'll dig into every lead. He must have left some trace."

Frank stood up, a renewed sense of purpose in his eyes. "Let's get to work. We're getting closer, but we have to stay vigilant. This bastard isn't going to slip through our fingers again."

As the team dispersed to their tasks, Frank couldn't help but feel a sense of urgency. They were on the right track, but with The Mathematician still at large, every moment counted. The hunt was far from over, but they were closing in on their prey, and this time, they wouldn't stop until they had him.

~TWENTY-NINE~

Tracking the Shadow

Frank Griffin paced the conference room, his mind racing with possibilities. With the revelation that Heinrich von Deusen had faked his death, the team was closer to unraveling the mystery, but finding him was another challenge entirely. They couldn't assume it was definitely von Deusen, but all signs pointed to him. They needed to figure out where he was hiding and what identity he was using.

"We can't just assume it's von Deusen," Frank began, addressing the team. "But given his history and the fact that he faked his death, it seems likely. The question is, where is he now?"

"Agreed," said Worthington. "We need to explore every possibility. Someone like him wouldn't just disappear without leaving some sort of trace."

Sarah Collins nodded, pulling out a map of Boston and its surrounding areas. "If he's still in Massachusetts, we need to narrow down the possibilities. Where would someone like von Deusen go? He'd need resources, a place to stay under the radar, and access to his academic interests."

Olivia chimed in, "Given his background in academia, he might have gravitated towards universities or research institutions. We should check faculty lists, recent hires, and visiting scholars in the Boston area over the last few years."

Frank nodded. "Good thinking. We'll start with local universities and expand our search from there."

The team divided up the tasks. Collins and Worthington began contacting universities and research institutions, looking for any new hires or guest lecturers with suspicious backgrounds. Frank and Olivia delved into public records, seeking any trace of von Deusen's new identity.

Days turned into weeks as they combed through databases, interviewed colleagues, and followed up on every lead. They encountered numerous dead ends and false leads, but slowly, a pattern began to emerge.

One evening, Collins burst into the conference room, her face alight with excitement. "I think I've got something! There's a visiting professor at MIT who fits the profile. He joined about a year ago, teaches advanced mathematics, and goes by the name Dr. Hans Breuer. His credentials check out, but there's something off about his background. It's almost too perfect."

Frank leaned in, his interest piqued. "Too perfect how?"

Collins explained, "His academic history is spotless, but it lacks depth. No personal details, no connections to colleagues outside of published papers. It's like he appeared out of nowhere."

Worthington nodded thoughtfully. "Could be a fabricated identity. If von Deusen was smart enough to fake his death, he's smart enough to create a believable new persona."

Olivia added, "We should check if Dr. Breuer has any unusual habits or behaviors. Maybe something that doesn't fit the usual academic profile."

The next day, Frank and Collins visited MIT to gather more information about Dr. Hans Breuer. They spoke with several faculty members and students, all of whom described Breuer as a brilliant but reclusive individual. He rarely socialized, kept to himself, and seemed almost paranoid about security.

One student mentioned, "He's always looking over his shoulder, like he's afraid someone's watching him. And he never talks about his past. It's weird for someone so accomplished."

Frank exchanged a glance with Collins. "It's worth looking into further. Let's see if we can find anything that ties him to von Deusen."

Back at the precinct, they dug deeper into Dr. Hans Breuer's history. Collins discovered that Breuer's credentials, while impressive, had all been established in the last few years. His references checked out, but many were from individuals who were either deceased or untraceable.

"This has to be him," Frank said, feeling a surge of determination. "But we need concrete proof before we can move in."

As the team compiled their findings, the picture became clearer. Dr. Hans Breuer had all the hallmarks of a fabricated identity. His expertise in mathematics, his secretive nature, and his sudden appearance in the academic world all pointed towards von Deusen.

Late one evening, Worthington called a meeting. "Based on everything we've uncovered, it's highly likely that von Deusen is hiding in plain sight as Dr.

Hans Breuer. He's right here in the Boston area, but we need to be sure before we make any moves."

Frank nodded. "We'll keep a close watch on him, gather more evidence, and when we're ready, we'll make our move. This time, we won't let him slip through our fingers."

The hunt was intensifying, and with each passing day, they were closing in on the man who had eluded them for so long. But the danger was far from over, and they knew that the final confrontation would be the most perilous yet.

~THIRTY-

Another Dead End

The tension in the precinct was palpable as Frank Griffin, Sarah Collins, and the rest of the team continued their surveillance on Dr. Hans Breuer. Weeks of painstaking investigation had led them to this man, and every detail seemed to point to him being the elusive von Deusen. But deep down, Frank couldn't shake a nagging doubt.

One evening, after another long day of watching Breuer's every move, Frank and Collins met with Captain Hogan to discuss their next steps.

"Captain," Frank began, "we've been watching Breuer for weeks now. He fits the profile, but something doesn't feel right. There's no solid evidence linking him to the murders."

Hogan frowned, rubbing his temples. "We can't afford to waste time on a dead end, Frank. We need results. What do you suggest?"

"I think it's time we bring him in for questioning," Frank replied. "See if we can get a confession or at least something to go on."

The following morning, Frank and Collins arrived at MIT. They found Dr. Hans Breuer in his office, surrounded by chalkboards covered in complex equations. Breuer looked up, startled, as they entered.

"Dr. Breuer," Frank said, showing his badge. "We need to ask you a few questions."

Breuer's eyes narrowed. "What is this about? I've done nothing wrong."

"We just need to clarify some details about your background," Collins said, trying to sound reassuring.

Reluctantly, Breuer followed them to the precinct. In the interrogation room, he sat across from Frank and Collins, his demeanor growing more defensive with each passing minute.

"Dr. Breuer," Frank began, "your academic history is impressive, but there are gaps. Can you explain why there's so little personal information available about you?"

Breuer's expression hardened. "I value my privacy. My work speaks for itself."

Collins leaned forward. "You've been very secretive, Dr. Breuer. We need to know why."

Breuer glared at them. "Is that a crime? I don't understand what you're insinuating."

Hours of questioning yielded nothing substantial. Breuer was evasive but not incriminating. Frustrated, Frank and Collins stepped out of the room to consult with Captain Hogan and Worthington.

"He's not giving us anything," Frank said, running a hand through his hair. "What if we're wrong about him?"

"Let's not jump to conclusions," Worthington replied. "We need more evidence before we can rule him out completely."

That evening, Olivia joined Frank at the precinct. "Any luck?" she asked, concern etched on her face.

Frank shook his head. "Nothing. Breuer's not budging, and I'm starting to think we've been barking up the wrong tree."

Olivia sighed. "We'll figure it out, Frank. We always do."

The next day, the team regrouped, pouring over every detail they had on Breuer. They scrutinized his movements, his interactions, and his past, but nothing concrete connected him to the murders.

Finally, Captain Hogan called a meeting. "We've hit a wall with Breuer. There's no evidence to hold him, and we can't justify keeping him any longer."

Frank clenched his fists in frustration. "So, we're back to square one?"

"Not entirely," Worthington said, a thoughtful look on his face. "We've eliminated a strong suspect. That's progress. We need to revisit our leads and see what we missed."

As they released Dr. Hans Breuer, Frank felt a heavy weight settle on his shoulders. They were no closer to catching The Mathematician, and the clock was ticking. Every moment they spent chasing false leads was another moment the real killer was out there, planning his next move.

Later that night, back at their new home, Olivia tried to comfort Frank. "We'll get him, Frank. You can't lose hope now."

"I know," Frank replied, his voice heavy with exhaustion. "But every dead end makes it harder to keep going."

Olivia took his hand. "We'll find him. Together."

Frank nodded, finding strength in her words. "Together."

As they settled in for the night, Frank's mind raced with possibilities. Somewhere out there, The Mathematician was watching, waiting. And Frank knew they had to be ready for whatever came next.

~THIRTY-ONE~

The Convergence Lead

In a meeting with Captain Hogan, his partner Collins, his now-fiancée Chief Medical Examiner Olivia Brooks, and the two detectives he could barely tolerate, Jake Thompson and Mike Reynolds. Since Griffin and Thompson's fight, they had reached an uneasy truce for the sake of the victims. Professionalism had to take precedence over personal animosities.

Frank stood at the head of the table, addressing the team. "With Lars Meier, Leopold Fischer, Brian Keller and Professor Albert Wilson all in prison awaiting trial, we should all be proud of a job well done. But, at the same time, not. These four were just pawns in The Mathematician's grand game of chess. Their murders, although heinous, didn't really fit the profile. They killed both men and women in various ways. They all have ties to a German background and Mathematics and are absolutely part of "The Order", but this will never stop until we cut off the head"

"The true Mathematician is a slayer. He kills with a blade, he writes his messages with the blood of his victim, he mutilates the body, then arranges them with fixed hair. In short, he's a deranged, sick fuck."

Captain Hogan nodded grimly. "We need to break Wilson. He's our best shot at getting closer to this bastard."

Collins leaned forward; her expression intense. "Do you think he'll talk?"

Frank exchanged a glance with Olivia, who gave a subtle nod. "He might. Wilson's smart but he's not the mastermind. We give him some time in jail to stew, then we offer him a deal for valuable information."

A few weeks later, the team was ready to confront Wilson. The interrogation room was cold and sterile, the kind of place designed to unnerve even the most composed individuals. Frank, Collins, and Olivia entered, ready to play their parts.

Albert Wilson sat at the metal table; his once neat appearance now disheveled. His eyes flicked up as the trio entered, showing a glimmer of recognition but no fear.

Frank began. "Professor Wilson, we need to talk. You've had some time to think things over. I'm sure you realize the situation you're in."

Wilson remained silent, his eyes narrowing slightly. Olivia stepped forward, her voice calm and authoritative. "Albert, we know you're not the mastermind. You're a pawn. But you can help yourself here. Give us something useful, and maybe we can work out a deal."

Wilson looked between them, weighing his options. He leaned back in his chair, exhaling slowly. "You want information about The Order of Pythagoras?"

"Yes," Collins said, her tone firm. "We need to know who's behind all this."

Wilson's lips twisted into a bitter smile. "You think I don't want to help myself? You think I'm enjoying this? The truth is, I don't know who the head of the Order is. No one does. He's a ghost, a phantom. All I know is that he's a mathematical genius with a plan that's far beyond our understanding."

Frank's frustration bubbled beneath the surface. "You've got to give us more than that, Wilson. We need something concrete."

Wilson sighed, rubbing his temples as if trying to dispel a headache. "I can tell you this much: He operates on a level of precision and logic that's terrifying. Every move is calculated, every decision purposeful. He communicates through a network of intermediaries, never revealing himself directly. The only name I ever heard was 'Pythagoras,' but that's obviously a code name."

Olivia leaned in, her eyes piercing. "What about the messages? The codes he leaves? How do they work?"

Wilson shook his head. "The codes... they're part of a larger puzzle, a mathematical construct that ties into everything he believes. He sees the world in numbers, in patterns. The murders, the codes—they're all pieces of a grand equation. He believes he can bring about some sort of radical change through his work. But what that change is, I don't know."

Frank felt a chill run down his spine. "So, you're telling us that he's got a grand plan, but you have no idea what it is or who he is?"

Wilson nodded slowly. "That's right. But there's one thing I can give you. There's a place—a sort of meeting point. It's where the lower members of the Order go to receive instructions. I was never high enough to know the exact location, but I've heard it's somewhere in the old industrial district. They call it 'The Convergence.'"

Collins scribbled down notes, her eyes wide with interest. "The Convergence. That's a start. We can work with that."

Frank felt a spark of hope. It wasn't much, but it was a lead. "Thank you, Wilson. This might just be the break we need."

As they left the interrogation room, Frank turned to his team. "We need to find this Convergence and shut it down. We're getting closer. Let's move."

Back at the precinct, the team gathered to discuss their next steps. The atmosphere was tense but charged with a new sense of purpose. They now had a direction, a place to focus their efforts.

~THIRTY-TWO~

The Courier's Secret

Captain Hogan addressed the group. "Alright, everyone. We've got a lead. We're going to scour the industrial district for this Convergence. We need to be thorough and discreet. This might be our only chance to get closer to The Mathematician."

Thompson and Reynolds, despite their rough history with Frank, nodded in agreement. "We're ready," Thompson said. "Let's bring this bastard down."

Over the next few days, the team worked tirelessly, combing through records, interviewing informants, and conducting surveillance in the industrial district. They followed every lead, no matter how small, piecing together the fragments of information they had.

One evening, as Frank and Olivia sat in his apartment, poring over maps and notes, Olivia reached out and took his hand. "We're getting closer, Frank. I can feel it."

Frank squeezed her hand, his eyes filled with determination. "We'll catch him, Olivia. And when we do, we can finally start our life together."

The search for The Convergence continued, and with each passing day, the team grew more focused, more driven. They knew they were closing in on The Mathematician, and they wouldn't stop until they had him in their grasp.

The next few weeks were a blur of long hours and relentless pursuit. The industrial district was vast and filled with abandoned buildings, each one a potential hideout. The team split into smaller groups, meticulously searching each location.

One day, Collins came rushing into the precinct, her face flushed with excitement. "I think I've found something," she said, holding up a piece of paper. "An old warehouse on the outskirts. It matches the description we got from one of our informants."

Frank and the others gathered around, studying the map. "This could be it," Frank said, his heart pounding. "We need to move fast."

They assembled a tactical team, preparing for a raid. The tension was palpable as they drove to the location, each member of the team focused and ready for whatever lay ahead.

As they approached the warehouse, Frank signaled for silence. They moved in, weapons drawn, ready to confront the unknown. The door creaked open, and they entered, sweeping the area with their flashlights.

The warehouse was dark and eerie, filled with shadows and the faint scent of decay. They moved cautiously, their footsteps echoing in the vast, empty space.

Suddenly, a figure darted out from behind a stack of crates. Frank and Thompson reacted instantly, giving chase. The figure was fast, but they were determined. They cornered him in a small office, blocking his escape.

"Stop right there!" Frank shouted, his gun trained on the suspect.

The man raised his hands, a look of fear in his eyes. "Don't shoot! I'm just a messenger. I don't know anything!"

Collins stepped forward, her voice firm. "Who are you? What do you know about The Order of Pythagoras?"

The man trembled, his fear palpable. "I'm nobody. They call me The Courier. I just deliver messages. Please, I don't know anything else."

Frank felt a surge of frustration. "We need information. Where is The Mathematician?"

The Courier shook his head frantically. "I don't know. I swear. They never tell me anything. I just pick up the messages and deliver them. That's all."

Olivia stepped forward, her voice calm and soothing. "Listen, we're not here to hurt you. We just need to find him. Can you help us in any way?"

The man hesitated, then nodded slowly. "There's a drop point, not far from here. It's where I pick up the messages. Maybe you can find something there."

Frank exchanged a glance with Collins and nodded. "Alright, take us there."

They followed The Courier to a rundown building a few blocks away. Inside, they found a hidden compartment filled with papers and coded messages. Frank felt a glimmer of hope as they gathered the evidence.

Back at the precinct, they worked tirelessly to decode the messages, piecing together the information they had. Slowly but surely, they began to see a pattern, a series of clues that pointed to The Mathematician's next move.

As they connected the dots, Frank felt a surge of determination. They were getting closer, and he knew they wouldn't stop until they had The Mathematician in their grasp.

The messages led them to a series of locations across the city, each one a piece of the puzzle. The Mathematician's network was intricate, and he was always one step ahead, but the team was relentless. They followed every lead, interviewed every informant, and analyzed every piece of evidence with meticulous care.

One evening, as Frank and Olivia sat in the precinct's conference room, poring over the latest decoded message, Frank looked up at Olivia. "We're getting closer. I can feel it. He's slipping up."

Olivia nodded, her eyes intense. "We have to be careful, though. He's dangerous and unpredictable. One wrong move, and we could lose everything."

Frank reached out and took her hand. "I know. But we're in this together. We'll catch him, and then we can finally start our life together."

Just then, Collins burst into the room, excitement in her eyes. "Frank, Olivia, I think I've got something. The latest message—it mentions a specific date and location. It looks like he's planning something big."

Frank and Olivia exchanged a glance. "When and where?" Frank asked, his heart pounding.

Collins pointed to the map on the wall. "Tomorrow night, at the old abandoned train station on the outskirts of town. It's heavily coded, but I'm sure of it. He's planning to meet someone there."

Frank stood up, his resolve hardening. "This is it. We need to be ready. We'll stake out the location and catch him in the act."

The team spent the rest of the day preparing for the operation. They coordinated with SWAT, set up surveillance, and planned their approach with military precision. Frank felt a mix of anticipation and anxiety, knowing that this could be their best chance to finally catch The Mathematician.

~THIRTY-THREE

Finality

As night fell, they moved into position around the train station. The old building was dark and foreboding, its shadowy form barely visible in the moonlight. The team moved silently, taking up their positions and waiting for any sign of movement.

Hours passed, the tension growing with each passing minute. Then, just after midnight, they saw a figure approaching the station. Frank signaled for silence, his heart racing. This was it.

The figure entered the building, and Frank and his team moved in, their guns drawn. They navigated the dark, labyrinthine corridors, their footsteps echoing softly in the eerie silence.

Suddenly, they heard voices. Frank motioned for his team to stop, straining to hear. The voices were coming from a room up ahead. He signaled for them to move in, slowly and carefully.

As they reached the door, Frank took a deep breath and kicked it open, his gun trained on the figures inside. "Freeze! Police!"

The figures turned, their faces a mix of surprise and fear. One of them, a tall man with sharp features and piercing eyes, stared at Frank with a cold, calculating gaze. Frank knew instantly that this was The Mathematician, Heinrich Van Deusen.

"Hands up!" Frank shouted, his voice steady.

The Mathematician raised his hands slowly, a sinister smile spreading across his face. "Well, well, Detective Griffin. I must say, I'm impressed. You've finally caught up to me."

Frank's eyes widened in shock and disbelief. "What the fuck? Wolfgang?! You're Heinrich Van Deusen ??"

The man standing before him, the mastermind behind the heinous murders, was none other than Professor Wolfgang Einstein. The brilliant mathematician who had been helping them decode the cryptic messages was, in fact, the very monster they had been hunting.

"Yes, Frank," Wolfgang replied, his voice dripping with condescension. "It's me. All this time, right under your nose."

Frank's mind raced, trying to reconcile the helpful, if eccentric, professor with the cold-blooded killer before him. "Why? Why would you do this?"

Wolfgang's smile faded, replaced by a cold, calculating expression. "Because, Frank, I see the world in a way that you cannot begin to comprehend. The Order of Pythagoras, the codes, the murders—they're all part of a grand design, a way to bring about a new understanding of reality. But you, with your simplistic notions of good and evil, could never understand."

Frank clenched his jaw, anger and betrayal boiling inside him. "You're insane, Wolfgang. This ends now."

Wolfgang's smile returned, more sinister than before. "Is it? Or is this just the beginning?"

Before Frank could react, there was a sudden explosion. The force of the blast threw him backward, the world spinning around him. He hit the ground hard, his ears ringing, the air thick with smoke and debris.

As he struggled to his feet, he saw Wolfgang fleeing through a side door. Ignoring the pain, Frank gave chase, his determination unwavering. He couldn't let him get away, not now.

The chase led them through the dark, winding streets of the industrial district. Frank pushed himself to the limit, his muscles burning, his breath ragged. He could see Wolfgang up ahead, his silhouette barely visible in the shadows.

Just as he was about to close the

gap, Wolfgang darted into an alley, disappearing from view. Frank followed, his heart pounding. As he rounded the corner, he saw Wolfgang climbing a fire escape, heading for the rooftops.

Frank followed; his every movement driven by sheer willpower. He climbed the fire escape, his hands gripping the cold metal, his eyes fixed on his target. As he reached the rooftop, he saw Wolfgang standing at the edge, his back to the city.

"It's over!" Frank shouted, his voice echoing in the night. "There's nowhere left to run."

Wolfgang turned slowly, his eyes gleaming with a mix of defiance and amusement. "You think you've won, Detective? This is far from over. My work will continue, with or without me."

Frank took a step forward, his gun trained on Wolfgang. "You're done. Surrender now."

Wolfgang smiled, a chilling, almost serene expression. "You're too late. The pieces are already in place. The game is far from over."

Before Frank could react, Wolfgang stepped backward, falling off the edge of the building. "Wolfgang, noooo!" Frank yelled, rushing to the edge. He watched in horror as Wolfgang plummeted to the ground below.

He stared in shock, his mind racing. Had it really ended this way? He felt a mix of relief and frustration, knowing that even in death, Wolfgang had managed to maintain control.

The rest of the team arrived moments later, their expressions a mix of concern and confusion. Olivia rushed to Frank's side, her eyes wide with worry. "Frank, are you okay?"

Frank nodded slowly, still staring at the spot where Wolfgang had fallen. "Yeah, I'm fine. It's just... it's over."

Olivia wrapped her arms around him, holding him close. "I'm so sorry, Frank. I know he was your friend. This must be devastating."

Frank hugged her back, feeling a mix of emotions. Relief, sadness, betrayal. It was over, but at what cost?

In the days that followed, they pieced together the remnants of Wolfgang's network. They arrested several key members of The Order of Pythagoras, dismantling the organization piece by piece. The city slowly began to heal, the shadow of fear lifting as justice was served.

Frank and Olivia's wedding was a small, intimate affair, attended by close friends and family. They stood together, exchanging vows, their love a beacon of hope amidst the darkness they had faced. As they kissed, sealing their commitment to each other, Frank felt a sense of peace he hadn't known in years.

In the months that followed, Frank and Olivia settled into their new life together. They traveled, explored new places, and cherished every moment they had. The scars of the past slowly faded, replaced by the promise of a brighter future.

Frank retired from the force, his years of service honored by his colleagues. He looked forward to a quieter life, filled with love and happiness. The memories of Wolfgang's reign of terror lingered, but they no longer held the same power over him.

One evening, as Frank and Olivia sat on their porch, watching the sunset, Frank took Olivia's hand, a smile playing on his lips. "We did it," he said softly. "We made it through."

Olivia leaned her head on his shoulder, her eyes shining with love. "Yes, we did. And now, we have the rest of our lives to look forward to."

As the sun dipped below the horizon, casting a warm, golden glow over them, Frank felt a sense of contentment wash over him. He had faced the darkness and emerged stronger, with the love of his life by his side. Together, they would face whatever the future held, their hearts forever intertwined.

Epilogue

The Mathematician, known by many names—Wolfgang Einstein, Heinrich van Deusen, —had survived the fall that was supposed to end his reign of terror. He had been caught after a harrowing chase, culminating in a desperate leap from a rooftop. The fall hadn't killed him, but it had shattered his body, breaking his back and a leg. The months of recovery that followed were excruciating, but the pain only served to deepen his resolve.

Now, confined to a wheelchair for the time being, he sat in the dimly lit cell that would be his home for the rest of his life. The court had sentenced him to 23 consecutive life sentences, a punishment that reflected the gravity of his crimes. The cell was stark and cold, its walls a drab gray that mirrored the emptiness of his existence. But his mind, as sharp as ever, was far from idle.

He spent hours each day contemplating the intricacies of his past, the elegance of his crimes, and the mistakes that had led to his capture. And always, his thoughts returned to one man: Detective Frank Griffin.

The relationship between the Mathematician and Griffin had been complex, a twisted dance of hunter and hunted. Griffin had retired shortly after the Mathematician's capture, his career marked by the relentless pursuit of a man who eluded capture and destroyed the lives of 23 victims and their families. Despite the retirement, the Mathematician knew deep down that their connection was far from severed.

One afternoon, the sound of approaching footsteps echoed through the prison corridor. The Mathematician's pulse quickened slightly—a rare occurrence. The door to his cell opened, and there stood Frank Griffin, who seemed older and more worn than the last time they had faced each other, but with the same determined glint in his eyes.

"Frank," the Mathematician greeted, a twisted smile playing on his lips. "I was wondering when you'd come."

Griffin stepped into the cell, his expression unreadable. "I had to see for myself. Make sure you were really here."

"Oh, I'm here," the Mathematician said, gesturing to his wheelchair. "Quite immobile, as you can see. But not inactive. Never inactive."

Griffin pulled up a chair and sat down, facing his old nemesis. "Why, Wolfgang? Heinrich? Whatever the hell your name is. Why did you do it?"

The Mathematician's smile widened. "Names are just labels, Frank. What matters is the essence. The pursuit of perfection. You, of all people, should understand the beauty of a finely crafted plan."

"There's no beauty in what you did," Griffin replied, his voice tinged with anger. "You destroyed lives. For what? Some delusion of grandeur?"

"Not delusion, Frank. Vision." The Mathematician leaned forward slightly, his eyes gleaming. "Every equation, every formula—it was all part of something greater. You were a part of it too. The only one who could truly appreciate the depth of my work."

Griffin shook his head, a bitter laugh escaping his lips. "You're insane. But you're right about one thing. We're not done. As long as you're alive, there's a chance you could try something. Hurt someone."

The Mathematician's smile faded, replaced by a look of intense curiosity. "And that, Frank, is why you'll keep coming back. To make sure I'm contained. To remind yourself that you won. But deep down, you know the truth."

Griffin stood, his face hardening. "The truth is, you're a monster. And monsters belong in cages."

He turned to leave, but paused at the door. "I'll be watching you, Wolfgang. Heinrich. Whatever name you go by next. Don't ever forget that."

As Griffin's footsteps receded, the Mathematician's smile returned. He wheeled himself to the small window that offered a narrow view of the sky. The bars cast long shadows on the floor, but he didn't mind. He thrived in the shadows.

"Until next time, Frank," he whispered to himself, the smile never leaving his lips. "Until next time."

Made in the USA
Middletown, DE
20 August 2024

59500293R00156